"I was wondering marrying me.*

Her words echoed in her ears. Spoken aloud, they sounded like lunacy, but there was no taking them back. "It wouldn't be forever. Just until I get Jamie," she added hurriedly.

The stunned expression on his face caused nausea to bubble in her throat. "You probably aren't interested. Forget I asked," she blurted out.

But Eric was surprised by his own attitude. She was wrong. He *was* interested. "Well, I did promise Jamie I'd do what I could," he muttered. But it wasn't Jamie he was thinking of as he rose. What he was thinking of was her in his bed. *Don't you think marrying a woman simply to bed her is a little extreme?* his inner voice argued.

"If you need a husband for a while, I can handle that."

Dear Reader,

The holiday season is a time for family, love...and miracles! We have all this—and more!—for you this month in Silhouette Romance. So in the gift-giving spirit, we offer *you* these wonderful books by some of the genre's finest:

A workaholic executive finds a baby in his in-box and enlists the help of the sexy single mom next door in this month's BUNDLES OF JOY, *The Baby Came C.O.D.*, by RITA Award-winner Marie Ferrarella. *Both* hero and heroine are twins, and Marie tells their identical siblings' stories in *Desperately Seeking Twin*, out this month in our Yours Truly line.

Favorite author Elizabeth August continues our MEN! promotion with *Paternal Instincts*. This latest installment in her SMYTHESHIRE, MASSACHUSETTS series features an irresistible lone wolf turned doting dad! As a special treat, Carolyn Zane's sizzling family drama, THE BRUBAKER BRIDES, continues with *His Brother's Intended Bride*—the title says it all!

Completing the month are *three* classic holiday romances. A world-weary hunk becomes *The Dad Who Saved Christmas* in this magical tale by Karen Rose Smith. Discover *The Drifter's Gift* in RITA Award-winning author Lauryn Chandler's emotional story. Finally, debut author Zena Valentine weaves a tale of transformation—and miracles—in *From Humbug to Holiday Bride*.

So treat yourself this month—and every month!—to Silhouette Romance!

Happy holidays,

Joan Marlow Golan
Senior Editor

Please address questions and book requests to:
Silhouette Reader Service
U.S.: 3010 Walden Ave., P.O. Box 1325, Buffalo, NY 14269
Canadian: P.O. Box 609, Fort Erie, Ont. L2A 5X3

ELIZABETH AUGUST

PATERNAL INSTINCTS

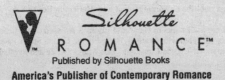

Silhouette

R O M A N C E™

Published by Silhouette Books

America's Publisher of Contemporary Romance

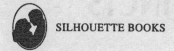

SILHOUETTE BOOKS

ISBN 0-373-19265-7

PATERNAL INSTINCTS

Copyright © 1997 by Elizabeth August

Printed in U.S.A.

ELIZABETH AUGUST

lives in western North Carolina, with her husband, Doug, and her three boys, Douglas, Benjamin and Matthew. She began writing romances soon after Matthew was born. She's always wanted to write.

Elizabeth does counted cross-stitching to keep from eating at night. It doesn't always work. "I love to bowl, but I'm not very good. I keep my team's handicap high. I like hiking in the Shenandoahs, as long as we start up the mountain so the return trip is down rather than vice versa." She loves to go to Cape Hatteras to watch the sun rise over the ocean. Elizabeth August has also published under the pseudonym Betsy Page.

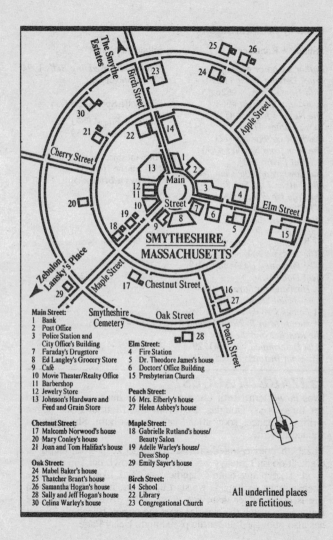

SMYTHESHIRE,
MASSACHUSETTS

Main Street:
1 Bank
2 Post Office
3 Police Station and
  City Office's Building
7 Faraday's Drugstore
8 Ed Langley's Grocery Store
9 Café
10 Movie Theater/Realty Office
11 Barbershop
12 Jewelry Store
13 Johnson's Hardware and
  Feed and Grain Store

Elm Street:
4 Fire Station
5 Dr. Theodore James's house
6 Doctors' Office Building
15 Presbyterian Church

Peach Street:
16 Mrs. Elberly's house
27 Helen Ashbey's house

Chestnut Street:
17 Malcomb Norwood's house
20 Mary Conley's house
21 Joan and Tom Halifax's house

Maple Street:
18 Gabrielle Rutland's house/
  Beauty Salon
19 Adelle Warley's house/
  Dress Shop
29 Emily Sayer's house

Oak Street:
24 Mabel Baker's house
25 Thatcher Brant's house
26 Samantha Hogan's house
28 Sally and Jeff Hogan's house
30 Celina Warley's house

Birch Street:
14 School
22 Library
23 Congregational Church

All underlined places
are fictitious.

Chapter One

Eric Bishop, code name Knight, lay in the hospital bed staring at the ceiling. Moving any part of his body required tremendous effort. He'd stopped drifting in and out of consciousness and was now fully awake. The images of Thistle and Coyote emerged from the foggy recesses of his mind. They were fellow covert agents working for The Unit, an elite squad of the military police, and they thought he was a traitor. He remembered telling them he was taking his orders from The Manager, their code for the head of The Unit, when the shooter had nailed him.

"They told me you'd woken."

Eric had been concentrating so hard on trying to recall the circumstances that had landed him in this hospital bed, he hadn't heard the approaching footsteps of the heavyset, elderly, very distinguished gentleman who now stood by his bedside in a well-tailored three-piece suit, leaning on a gold-topped cane. "Tobias." His gaze shifted to the rest of the room, scanning it quickly to make certain they were alone. Then in lowered tones he asked, "How are Thistle and Coyote?"

"They're fine," Tobias Smith replied, his manner fatherly.

In spite of his weakened condition, Eric managed a defiant scowl. "They think I'm a traitor. I'm not."

Tobias smiled reassuringly. "We all know that. Susan Irving was the mole. She told you The Manager wanted you to fake your death and go out into the cold with her as your only contact."

"Yes. I assumed she was relaying orders like always. They were coded."

"She broke the code."

Picturing the pretty blonde with such innocent eyes, Eric wondered if he was hallucinating. "She was the mole?"

"Never underestimate a secretary or a receptionist." Tobias repeated the lesson he'd learned.

"Did you catch her?"

"Yes." Tobias frowned as if displeased with himself. "After she was caught, she kept offering to cut a deal. At first, we refused. Fear for her safety had caused her to give us information that helped nail one of her cohorts in Mexico and we figured she didn't have much else to bargain with. Then she told us there was a man who'd taught her how to run her operation. In return, she'd paid him a percentage of the profits. She gave us the account number she'd put the money in, but it had been cleaned out about the time you'd gotten shot."

"Guess he was worried she wasn't covering her trail well enough and decided to sever his ties," Eric muttered.

Tobias nodded. "Most likely. According to her, she wasn't his only pupil. She was certain he had others he'd taught and continued to deal with. She also suspected that he sometimes ran an operation himself just for the kicks.''

"A mastermind who trains thieves and traitors. Nice guy," Eric said.

The frown on Tobias's face deepened. "She wouldn't give us the name until the deal was struck. Before that could happen, in spite of the security that was provided, she was poisoned. One of her guards had sold out for half a million dollars. He was found dead a couple of days later with a bullet in the head."

"And you never found out who she was going to name?"

Tobias shook his head. "I'm not even certain this mastermind she described exists. She could have emptied out that account herself and was creating a fictitious bad guy because she knew she needed something dramatic with which to deal. As to who paid for her death, she'd dealt with a lot of ruthless men, any of whom would have been afraid she might give evidence against them." His frown faded, replaced by an expression of concern. "Enough about Susan. How are you feeling?"

"As if I've been asleep for a year."

"Actually, it's been nearly three years."

Eric stared at Tobias in disbelief. This had to be one of those realistic nightmares. He ordered himself to wake up. Nothing changed.

"You were shot," Tobias reminded him.

"That I remember."

"The bullet did a lot of damage. You were operated on. While you were in intensive care, another attempt was made on your life. The doctor was instructed to make up a fake death certificate and then we had you transported to this private clinic. We were warned that transporting you could be dangerous but felt it was necessary in order to keep you alive. During transport you slipped into a coma. To be honest, when the nurse walked in this morning and found you awake, it was a shock to the staff here. They'd given up on you.'' Tobias grinned. ''But I hadn't. Tenacity was one of the major traits I looked for when recruiting my people.''

Eric was still having trouble comprehending this news. ''Three years?'' He suddenly frowned, recalling that Harold had taken over Tobias's position as head of The Unit before all of this had happened. ''Why are you here? I thought you'd retired...vanished from the game.''

''I'm doing a friend a favor.''

Mentally, Eric gave himself a slap on the head. Of course Harold wouldn't have come himself and risked exposing himself and one of his people.

''We think all of the loose ends have been cleaned up,'' Tobias said. ''But it would help if you could tell me about your activities during the weeks prior to your being shot.''

''I've been trying to remember, but I'm drawing a blank. The truth is my memory is pretty spotty for the two or three years before I was shot. I guess I remember Susan because I was about to tell Thistle and Coyote she was my contact. The doc says that it's not unusual for me to remember the very last things that were on my mind. He also says I might not get all of my memory back, and if I do, it'll probably be in bits and pieces.''

''Susan was very crafty. I doubt you discovered anything of any importance during the time you were being manipulated by her. Following your transfer from the hospital to here, there were a few inquiries made to determine if you were actually dead, but they ceased immediately after her capture. That makes me think that she was the only one worried about what you could reveal. You just work on getting your strength back. When you have, I'll return." Rising, Tobias frowned critically as his gaze traveled over Eric's lean form. "Your old wardrobe won't fit. I'll arrange for some sweat suits and tennis shoes to be provided for you until you're ready to leave here. Then you can do your own shopping."

Eric watched him leave. *Three years.* He'd lost three years of his life. "Looks like I have some catching up to do."

"Forty," Eric counted under his breath, completing another push-up. It was four weeks since he'd returned to the world of the living. His muscle tone was improving, but he still wasn't up to his full potential. Normally he could have done a hundred before tiring. Currently, fifty was his limit. When he finished this warm-up, he'd go through his katas, retraining his body to make the defensive karate moves with a sharpness that would hopefully keep him alive when he returned to the field.

Sensing he was being watched, he paused in the raised position and looked covertly toward the door. The polished leather shoes and gold-tipped cane told him who his visitor was. In one lithe movement he was on his feet. "I hope you've come to spring me from this place."

"I have," Tobias confirmed.

Half an hour later Eric sat beside his former superior in the rear seat of a rented luxury sedan. The blond man behind the wheel had been introduced to him as Tobias's grandnephew, Hagen Scanlon.

"Your doctor insists you be given a couple more months off duty to regain your full strength. You'll have it," Tobias said as the sedan pulled away from the private clinic. "After that you have two options. You can return to active duty in the military or take an early retirement and return to civilian life. If you choose the latter, I'd like you to consider coming to work for me. I'm running a private investigative agency now."

Eric grinned wryly. "Since returning to The Unit isn't one of those options, can I assume Harold is worried that I've lost my edge and will endanger his operation?"

"We're all aware that a close brush with death can affect a man, change his outlook. He might let fear rule, bolt too quickly…make mistakes."

"And you're not worried about that?"

"I know you. You're too responsible to knowingly endanger anyone. If you've lost your edge, you'll tell me."

Eric heard the question in Tobias's voice. "I don't think I've lost it. I'd still like to save the world from the bad guys."

Tobias nodded his approval. "However, as for The Unit, Harold's worry about you losing your edge isn't the only reason that isn't an option. Susan compromised its operation. It has been relocated and restaffed."

Recalling how protective both Tobias and Harold were toward their people, Eric nodded his understanding.

"So, now you know your options," Tobias continued in businesslike tones. "Consider them. In the meantime you need a place to recuperate." He extracted a large manila envelope from a nearby briefcase and handed it to Eric. "When you showed no signs of coming out of the coma, I had myself appointed your legal guardian. I canceled the lease on your apartment and had your furniture and personal effects put into storage." He named a storage company and a location just outside Washington, D.C. "The key to your private storage lock-up is in there." He nodded toward the envelope. "There is also your savings account book, your checkbook, a current credit card and an ATM card. The military wouldn't keep you on full salary. They wanted something to defer your medical costs. However, since the balance in your checking and savings accounts was fairly high, I had all new monies invested and they've paid off nicely. Currently, Hesper Lawton, my personal financial advisor, is overseeing your account. Her name and phone number are in there, and when you want access to any of those funds, just contact her.''

Eric frowned. "I had a designated amount each month being sent to the O'Malley Home for Boys."

"I saw that that was continued in full." Concern entered Tobias's voice. "However, three months ago I received notification that the O'Malley account had been closed. I'd been having your mail forwarded to me. A few days later a letter arrived from a Roxanne Dugan, informing you of Maude O'Malley's death and the closing of the home. It's all in that envelope."

Eric felt as if he'd been kicked in the stomach. Maude O'Malley wasn't blood kin and, other than the money he'd sent regularly, he hadn't seen her in years. Still, she was the closest to family he had.

"My jet is at the airport. I'll drop you and Hagen off in Washington, D.C., so you can renew your driver's license and buy some more clothes. And, if you want, you can get your car out of storage. It's at the same place as your other belongings. After that, I'd like for you to come up to my place to recuperate. Hagen will show you the way. It's right outside of Craftsbury Common, Vermont. The mountain air will do you good and the quiet will give you time to think about your future," Tobias continued.

"I'll want to make a stop in Pennsylvania," Eric said around the lump in his throat. "I need to pay my respects to Maude."

Tobias nodded.

They had reached the airport. After boarding the plane

and buckling himself into his seat, Eric leaned back, closed his eyes and recalled Maude O'Malley as he'd first seen her. She was medium in build, standing around five feet six inches tall, with flaming red hair lightly streaked with gray, and green eyes. He doubted that any woman had more spirit than her. The O'Malley Home for Boys had been born because of that spirit.

Maude's husband, Norman, had died, leaving her alone with the farm to run. She'd been in her mid-thirties at the time and determined to keep the place. When it came around to harvest time, she couldn't find help. She'd grown up in Eric's neighborhood. It was a blue-collar enclave in Philadelphia that had fallen on hard times. She went back there looking for some sturdy teenage boys to hire for a month.

"All the good'uns done gone," one of the older women had told her. "All's we got left is the troublemakers and loafers."

"Then I'll take what's left," Maude had said. She'd found four boys to take back with her. Two went home almost immediately when they discovered how much work was involved. But two had stayed until the crop was in.

Later that winter one of the boys who had remained came back and asked if he could stay and work for his room and board. His mother had taken off and his father was in jail. Maude, never having had any children of her own, welcomed him like a long-lost son. The second boy who had stayed had such an improved attitude, his juvenile probation officer came out to the farm to visit Maude. She suggested a couple of boys Maude could hire for the next summer...boys the officer felt had potential for good but needed to get out of their current environment, even if it was just for a short while.

As the years passed more boys came to stay. Sometimes it was the juvenile authorities who recommended Maude's place to families as an alternative to the child ending up in jail. Sometimes, a parent or guardian heard about the farm through word of mouth and brought a child they could no longer handle. Or sometimes, as in Eric's case, an unwanted child was dropped off at the gate with a note giving Maude guardianship.

The rules were simple. You worked. You went to church. You didn't steal and you didn't hurt anyone. In return Maude gave the boys love and the feeling that they were members of a real family. She never expected perfection. But if you crossed her, she had a way of looking at you with so much disappointment in her eyes that you wanted to crawl under a rock.

"Maude O'Malley must have meant a great deal to you," Tobias said, breaking into Eric's thoughts.

Eric didn't normally feel comfortable talking about himself, but the memories of his childhood were too strong at the moment. They demanded to be released. "My mother died when I was born. My father was an alcoholic and physically abusive. My mother's family didn't want to have anything to do with him or me. My dad had beaten my mother the night before she went into labor. He didn't want to face up to the fact that he was probably responsible for her death, so he blamed me. He took me directly from the hospital to his parents and left me with them. They weren't happy about having another child to raise. I was getting into trouble with the police by the time I was nine. When I was ten, my grandmother heard about Maude's place and had my father sign a paper giving Maude guardianship of me. Then they took me out there and dropped me off. The authorities warned Maude not to keep me. They said I was incorrigible and they

doubted I was redeemable. But Maude kept me. We had
a few rough times those first months, but she proved to
me that there were good people in this world.''

"I wish I'd known her," Tobias said.

Eric nodded, then fell silent once again. He hadn't seen
Maude in years. The first Christmas after he'd left, he'd
gone back, but it hadn't been the same. She'd had her
hands full with a new nine-year-old who reminded him
of himself and a fifteen-year-old who'd been badly
abused. Eric had known she was glad to see him, but he
also knew that, like the baby bird pushed from the nest,
he didn't belong there anymore.

After that, he'd called once in a while when he needed
to hear a friendly voice and he'd sent money regularly,
but he hadn't gone back. As the plane touched down in
Washington, D.C., he said, "There's no need for Hagen
to baby-sit me. I'll find my way to your place on my
own."

For a moment Tobias looked as if he was going to
argue, then, reaching into his pocket, he took out a gold
case and extracted a business card from it. "This has my
phone number on it. Call me if you need me."

Eric thanked him and, after shoving the manila envelope into his satchel, he disembarked.

Roxanne Dugan, known as Roxy, took the intricately
carved wooden box from its drawer and set it on the table.
Seating herself, she opened it and took out the deck of
Tarot cards housed within. For as many generations as
anyone could remember, the women in her family had
read cards. This deck had been handmade by her great-
grandmother and given to Roxy as a gift on the day she
was born. She loved the artwork and the feel of them. In

her younger, more skeptical days, she'd discounted their warnings and had lived to regret it.

It had been several months since she'd sought their guidance. Her chin trembled as she recalled the last time she'd laid them out. It had been just after Maude's heart attack. She'd gone to them hoping they would tell her that Maude would be all right. Instead, they'd told her that Death was at the door. Hating them because they were the messengers of news she knew was true but didn't want to face, she'd put them away and had not wanted to look at them again.

But for the past couple of weeks a sense of uneasiness had been building within her and she needed to know its cause. Hesitantly, she began to spread the cards. Jamie's card turned up first. Tears welled in her eyes. By the time Maude's heart had given out completely, she'd found safe sanctuary for all the children under Roxy's and her care except for the withdrawn ten-year-old. Roxy had tried to explain to the social services people that the boy needed to stay with her, that he was beginning to respond to her, but they'd explained that the law wouldn't allow that and had assured her that they would take good care of him. She'd told them that she wanted to adopt him and they'd told her that they didn't feel she could meet the required conditions. They'd even refused to tell her where he was. They'd said that he needed to make a complete break from her so that he could bond with his new family.

She knew the laws were made to protect the children and that the social services people were doing their best, but in Jamie's and her case they were wrong. At least, that's what she wanted to believe. Maybe the cards were telling her what she wanted them to tell her. She touched the card lovingly and said a silent prayer that a guardian angel was looking over the boy.

The next card brought a puzzled frown to her face. For approximately three years now The Hanged Man card had been one of the first two cards in any rotation. She'd given up trying to figure out why. Her instinct was to interpret it as a life in suspension. But that didn't describe her life, at least not until Jamie had been taken from her. Tonight, however, it was the Knight of Swords that appeared.

"I could use a knight in shining armor," she muttered. But she'd stopped believing in such myths a long time ago. Still, a glimmer of hope began to glow. The uneasiness she'd been feeling did resemble the kind of sensation a person experienced when waiting for something to happen or someone to arrive.

The next card extinguished the glimmer of hope. "The Lovers' card." The words left a bitter taste in her mouth. That card had no place in her life anymore. The deck was lying or playing games or merely being uncooperative. She gathered up the cards. "You're mad because you feel neglected," she accused them. "Well, if you continue to give me fairy tales, then you'll be gathering dust for a long time more." She shuffled the deck and dealt the cards once again.

The first two were the Knight of Swords and the Lovers' cards. Scowling, she again gathered up the rest without looking and shoved them back in the box.

Chapter Two

Turning his car onto the long dirt driveway that led to the farmhouse that had once belonged to Maude O'Malley, Eric was surprised by the feeling of homecoming that swept through him. With Maude gone, he'd expected a sense of emptiness. A little earlier, in the cemetery, standing beside her grave, he'd experienced sadness and a hollow sensation. He'd almost skipped coming to the house, but some force from within had insisted his pilgrimage would not be complete without seeing the old homestead one last time.

Drawing nearer, he saw a woman in jeans and a shirt on a ladder scraping paint. Her long brown hair was tied back with a bandanna. She was medium in build with curves in all the right places. Noticing his car, she stopped working and, as he parked, began to descend. Her movements were awkward. Worried that she might fall, he climbed out of the car and hurried toward her. But she was on the ground safely before he reached her.

Roxy's gaze traveled over the blond, blue-eyed

stranger. She judged his age to be in the early to mid-thirties. He looked pale and thin. His jeans and shirt were new. She could tell that because the jeans looked stiff and the button-down shirt still had crisp creases left from the factory folds. *Probably one of Maude's former boys who just got out of prison and has come looking for a handout or redemption,* she mused acidly. Most of Maude's boys had turned out well, but a few had been rotten apples, and they'd caused Maude a lot of grief by coming here with sad stories and conning her out of money she couldn't afford to give. One had even used the farm to hide out from the police. But this one was going to learn that she wasn't as forgiving nor as naive as Maude had been.

Eric judged the woman's age to be near thirty. She was no raving beauty, but she would have been pleasant to look at if her expression hadn't been so inhospitable. Those cold brown eyes of hers had probably intimidated many a man, he guessed. "I didn't mean to interrupt your work. I just wanted to drop by to see the place for old times' sake."

"It's not much to look at." Roxy's shoulders squared with pride. "But I'm working on it."

Eric's gaze left her to view the huge old two-story farmhouse. It was in dire need of painting and the chimney needed repointing. One of the front windows was boarded over and the screen door was covered with patches. "Maude used to keep this place in great shape."

Roxy's gaze turned colder. "Money for major repairs has been pretty scarce the past few years. And now that Maude isn't here anymore and neither are any of the boys, I have to do the work myself and hold down a full-time job in town."

Realizing he'd offended her, Eric mentally kicked himself. He definitely needed to work on his people skills.

"Sorry. I didn't mean anything critical by that. It just hurts to see it this way."

Roxy knew what he meant and her flare of anger died. "Yeah. Well, eventually it'll look better." Jamie's small, trusting face filled her mind. "But that's not going to happen if I stand around talking to you. If you've come looking for a handout, there's nothing to give. If you've come looking for Maude she's..." Her throat constricted, refusing to say the word *dead.* "She's at rest."

Eric saw the flash of pain in the woman's eyes. She'd obviously cared a great deal for Maude. "I know. I received a letter from a Roxanne Dugan."

Roxy's gaze narrowed on her visitor. During Maude's last days, she'd given Roxy a very short list of names and asked her to write them letters of thanks for their support during the years. Roxy had known all of them except for one. "I'm Roxanne Dugan."

Eric extended his hand. "I'm Eric Bishop."

Mentally Roxy put a check by that name on the list. That was the one she hadn't known anything about except what Maude had told her, and that hadn't been much. He'd been one of Maude's boys. After he left the farm he'd become a career man in the military and had been stationed all over the world, but he'd never forgotten the farm, and he sent checks regularly. Accepting the handshake, Roxy was startled by the pleasure the contact caused...it carried a feel of warmth and security. "I'm sorry I was so brisk. A few of Maude's former boys came back to take advantage of her. The trouble some of them caused has left me suspicious of strangers," she said as he released her hand.

Eric nodded his understanding, then his gaze shifted back to the house. "I would have come sooner to pay my respects but I've been in the hospital. I only just read your letter yesterday.''

His paleness and new clothes took on a new meaning. ''Your stay must have been a long one.''

''I was in a coma for three years,'' he replied absently, continuing to frown at the farmhouse. It was as if all that was good from his youth had been destroyed.

Roxy bit back a gasp. *A life in suspension...The Hanged Man!* Glad his attention was elsewhere, she quickly regained her composure. ''I'm sorry.''

Trained never to miss anything, Eric had noticed her momentary show of shock, but then he was still a bit stunned by the fact that he'd lost three years of his life. ''Are you planning to reopen the Home when you get the house back into shape?''

Roxy looked over her shoulder at the massive job ahead of her. ''No. Maude willed the property to me, but she *was* the O'Malley Home for Boys.'' Her chin tightened defensively. ''The donations to keep the place going came in because of her. Most were from locals and they made it clear to me that once Maude was gone, they wouldn't support the Home any longer. Besides, the donations weren't enough to cover the bills and Maude refused to become part of the foster care system. She wanted the boys who came to be able to stay without the worry of being suddenly uprooted at the whim of some bureaucrat. I got a job in town to pay what the donations didn't cover. But, with Maude gone, I couldn't keep this place going on my salary alone. Besides, there'd be no one to supervise the boys while I was at work.''

''What happened to the boys who were here?''

Tears burned at the back of Roxy's eyes. ''For the past three or four years, most of the boys Maude took in were from decent, hardworking families who were going through difficult times. The agreement Maude had made with them was that they would take their children back when they could provide for them. For those children, going back to their families presented a hardship but they were welcomed. There was one, Jamie Jordon, however, who'd been left here by his grandmother with a paper giving Maude guardianship.''

Eric had a harsh flashback to his own youth.

Swallowing back the lump that had formed in her throat, Roxy continued stiffly, "I tried to keep him. I figured I could look after one child just fine. But the social services people took him. They said they could better care for him.''

Eric's gaze had shifted back to her. "You don't sound convinced.''

"I'm not. Jamie was a special case. I'm hoping when I get this place back into shape, they'll reconsider and let me adopt him.''

Eric had planned to come here, say his goodbyes and be on his way. But he'd always found it difficult to turn his back on a damsel in distress and there was a sorrow in Roxanne Dugan's eyes that made her look very much like a woman in need of assistance. "I've got a couple of months of recuperating before I'm expected back on duty. Looks like you could use some help here.''

Roxy recalled her Tarot cards—the Hanged Man had been replaced by the Knight of Swords. Had the cards been trying to tell her that Eric Bishop would arrive to help her? Events in her life had caused her to develop a strong sense of independence. Accepting aid, even that freely offered, did not come easily. But she wouldn't be accepting help for herself, she argued. It was Jamie who was important, and anyone who could help her regain custody of the boy should be welcomed. She glanced back at the house. Besides, she was getting desperate. There was so much left to do, and with each passing day her concern for the child grew stronger. "I can't pay you, but I can offer you room and board."

"Accepted." Eric held his hand out to her.

As they shook on this deal, she was again aware of the warmth of his touch, and the image of The Lovers' card popped into her mind. Silently, she mocked herself. No man would be interested in her once they got a close look. If that card proved to be right, it would be nothing more than a one-night stand and she doubted they'd get past the disrobing stage. *I don't intend to get past the handshake stage!* she growled at herself. Angry that her mind had even traveled along this path, she shoved these thoughts out. "You can choose any room on the second floor to bunk in. There are bed linens in the hall closet and, if you're hungry, there's sandwich makings in the refrigerator. I need to get back to work."

Eric noticed her limp as she turned back to the ladder. "Should you be climbing with that injured leg?"

She glanced back at him. "It's an old injury. I'm used to maneuvering with it."

The sharp edge in her voice warned that this wasn't a subject for conversation and he said no more. Returning to the car to retrieve his satchel, he noticed a lingering warmth on his hand. A curious effect from a woman who clearly had no interest in him other than as a day laborer to aid her in her project, he thought. Deciding that the sensation was due merely to an emotional reaction to being back here at the farm, he grabbed his bag and went inside.

Upstairs, he automatically headed for the room he'd once occupied. He'd expected to experience at least a twinge of melancholy. Instead a feeling of being where he belonged swept through him. Dropping his satchel on the floor, he found the bed linens and made up one of the two twin beds in the room. Not taking the time to do any unpacking, he stripped out of his shirt and hung it in the closet. Then he put on a T-shirt. He intended to go directly outside and begin working, but he couldn't resist making a quick inspection of the rest of the house. He strode through the rooms he'd played and worked in when he was younger. The walls and ceilings had a fresh coat of paint and the woodwork and hardwood floors were polished and dustless. Clearly, Ms. Dugan had been working hard to restore the place.

Reminding himself that he was there to help, he went to the barn and found a ladder.

An hour later Roxy looked to the far end of the house. She'd had Eric start there and work toward her. He hadn't taken a break and she was beginning to worry about him. She told herself that he was an adult and would know how to pace himself, but she didn't buy this reasoning. Some men felt they had to push themselves to live up to their macho image. "How about stopping for something to eat and drink?" she called out. "I haven't had any lunch yet. I started working as soon as I got home from church."

Eric nodded and started down his ladder. He was in the kitchen washing his hands when she entered.

"You don't have to keep up with me," she said sternly. "I haven't spent the past several years in a hospital."

Eric grimaced self-consciously. He had been pushing himself, but then that was his nature. "I want to prove I can earn my keep."

The grimace had produced two long dimples in his cheeks. He was a handsome man, Roxy admitted, experiencing an attraction she'd sworn never to feel again.

Jerking her gaze away from him, she busied herself washing up. "You don't need to prove it in a day."

Eric caught the softened color in her eyes followed by the tightening of her jaw as she turned away. He recognized the behavior. She didn't want to like him, at least not too quickly. Something had happened to her to teach her to distrust people, or maybe just men. He couldn't be certain which. As she finished washing up and began taking sandwich makings out of the refrigerator, he noticed the tired lines in her face. "Looks like I'm not the only one who might be overworking myself."

Roxy made no response to his observation. Instead she nodded toward the array. "Help yourself. Would you like lemonade or water to drink?"

"Lemonade," he replied, then began making his sandwich.

Roxy nodded and forced her mind to remain on the food and the drinks. When her sandwich was ready and the drinks poured, she carried her lunch out onto the back porch and sat down in Maude's rocking chair.

Respecting her silence, Eric, too, had said nothing more while he made his sandwich. Following her outside, he seated himself on the stoop, as he had when he was a kid, and leaned against one of the pillars supporting the porch roof. The sound of the rocker brought back memories...some good, some bad...but then, a real home was like that. Only fantasies could be perfect.

In her mind's eye Roxy saw Jamie...slender, dark haired, a haunted expression on his face, sitting in the tire swing suspended from the branch of the old oak in the middle of the yard. "I've had trouble sleeping since they took Jamie away, so when I'm home, I work on repairing this house until I'm so exhausted all I can do is sleep."

Suddenly realizing she'd spoken aloud, she flushed and clamped her mouth shut.

Eric heard the love in her voice. "How often do you get to see him?"

"I don't." Hot tears again burned at the back of her eyes. "They won't even tell me where he is. They say he won't learn to relate to other people if he's still attached to me. But he wouldn't even relate to Maude...only me. I can't stop picturing him sitting alone in a corner somewhere, frightened and feeling deserted."

Her pain disturbed him. "Maybe he's found another child to play with," Eric suggested, trying to ease her mind.

"I doubt it. He won't talk. He prefers to keep to himself and there's a haunted look on his face that makes other children nervous. They tend to avoid him." She hadn't had anyone to talk to since Maude's death, and she needed to talk. "When he was six, he saw his father, in a drunken jealous rage, kill his mother and then himself. The father's jealousy was because he thought Jamie wasn't really his son. Jamie's maternal grandmother took him in, but she didn't honestly want him. No one wanted him. She saw his father in him and his father's family blamed him for the deaths. He withdrew into himself. According to the grandmother, he stopped speaking the night of the murder-suicide and to everyone's knowledge, he hasn't spoken since. About a year after the tragedy the grandmother heard about Maude's place and brought him out here. She refused to even come in. She stood on the porch and handed Maude a handwritten note giving Maude complete guardianship over the boy, then she told Maude that if Maude didn't want to keep him, she could turn him over to the authorities because she was tired of taking care of him."

Eric recalled his own childhood before he'd been brought to Maude's farm. "It's tough growing up unwanted."

"It's always tough being unwanted no matter what age you are." Roxy clamped her mouth shut. She'd assured herself a million times that she was over the pain. Obviously, she'd been lying to herself. But her private hell was her own and would remain her own.

"Sounds like you've had some experience," Eric noted.

"Life is full of experiences. As Maude used to say, the trick is to learn from them and move on." Uncomfortable with the path this conversation had taken, Roxy said, "It's time to eat and then get to work."

The bitter edge in her voice confirmed Eric's assessment that something had happened to Ms. Dugan that had scarred her deeply. But the hard set of her jaw let him know that whatever it was, she wasn't going to talk about it.

Later, back on his ladder, he wondered what her story was. *None of my business is what it is.* He was here to do some thinking about his own life, not stick his nose into someone else's, especially when that someone didn't want it there.

Chapter Three

Eric switched off the lamp on the table beside his bed and lay on his back staring into the dark. Although he was supposed to be settled in for the night, he was still dressed in his jeans, T-shirt and socks. His hostess's image was strong in his mind. She'd told him to call her Roxy and the name fit. Living with her was a lot like living with a block of granite. He'd been at the farm for four days. It had been a Sunday when he arrived. Beginning on Monday, Roxy went into town to work each day. She'd be gone from six-thirty to three-thirty or four. When she arrived home, she'd prepare dinner. While it was cooking, she'd inspect the work he'd done that day. Then they'd eat and work on the house until dark. After that, they'd have a snack and go to bed.

She was like a robot that went about its business on its own and expected others to behave in the same fashion. Even during mealtimes she rarely talked. It appeared that she'd told him all she was willing to relate to him on Sunday and had little else to say. She wasn't unfriendly.

But she made it clear by her actions and her body language that she didn't want to be his friend, either. It was as if she'd constructed a barrier around herself and he was not allowed past it.

Since Sunday, everything he'd discovered about her was from observation and tidbits she felt necessary to tell him. So far, he knew she worked at the local grocery store as a cashier, that she'd come to the farm about five years earlier and that she did have family in Philadelphia.

The part about the family he'd learned because of a series of phone calls on Tuesday night. From what he'd heard of the conversation with her first caller, he'd realized she was talking to her mother. He'd gathered that the woman wanted Roxy to sell the farm and move back home or get a house or apartment nearer her parents. The firm set of his hostess's jaw had told him that her mother was wasting her breath.

A few minutes later the phone had rung again. This time the caller had been her grandmother. Since she'd addressed the caller only as Grandmama, he didn't know if it was her paternal or maternal grandparent, but he guessed it was better than a fifty-fifty chance it was her maternal grandparent, since they spoke of her mother's call.

Again Roxy had held firm to her determination to remain on the farm and he'd begun to wonder why. If she sold the place, she could buy something smaller but in much better condition and probably have a little cash left over. Surely a more financially stable position would aid her in getting the boy back. Then his question had been answered.

"Even if the social services people insist on keeping us apart, someday he'll come looking for me and I want to be here," she'd said. Her jaw had hardened even more, and he'd had the feeling she was holding back a flood of tears. "I know he'll come."

The conviction in her voice had apparently convinced her grandmother that she could not be dissuaded, because there had been no further discussion of her selling the farm.

His mind returned to the present as the sound of a door being quietly opened caught his attention. It was followed by softly padded footfalls coming his way. They paused outside his door, then turned toward the stairs and grew faint as they descended to the first floor.

Each night he'd been here, his hostess had followed this same routine. In about half an hour or so, she'd return to her room and settle in for the night. The first couple of nights he'd been too tired to really think about her actions. Only the many years when his life had depended on him always being aware of his surroundings so that, even when asleep, he would wake instantly to any sounds of movement had caused him to wake enough to realize she'd risen. But he'd sensed no danger and, assuming she was a worrier and merely double-checking to make certain all the doors were locked, he'd gone back to sleep.

Last night, however, when they'd come upstairs, he'd made a point of mentioning that they were securely locked in. Still, about half an hour after they'd retired, she'd gotten up and gone downstairs. That was when he'd asked himself why she stopped by his door and listened for a moment as if to reassure herself that he was asleep. If she was merely checking the locks, what difference would it make if he was awake or asleep?

All day that question had bothered him. He'd told himself that what she did on her nightly rounds didn't matter. But in spite of the distance she was obviously determined to keep between them, he found himself more and more intrigued by Roxy Dugan. He wanted to know more about her. Curiosity could be a dangerous thing where this woman was concerned, he'd warned himself. Her attachment to the boy Jamie continued to make a strong impression on him. He could begin to feel a commitment he didn't want to feel. He was a loner and he planned to stay that way. But he hadn't heeded his warning, and tonight he would have his answer to what she was up to.

Slipping out of bed, he made his way quietly downstairs. There was light coming from the small room that had been Maude's private parlor. Remaining in the shadows, he looked inside. The light was being provided by a small lamp on a round table in a corner of the room. Roxy was seated at the table shuffling a deck of oversize cards. As she laid them out and began to turn them over, surprise registered on Eric's face.

"I would never have pictured you as the fortune-teller type," he said, emerging from his hiding place.

Roxy's gaze jerked to him. His skin had taken on a healthy glow and the T-shirt showed off the strength building in his arms and shoulders. Embers long dead within her began to glow with life. Allowing herself to feel any attraction to him was only going to lead to pain, she warned herself curtly. Aloud she said frostily, "I thought you were asleep."

"I got thirsty," he lied, not wanting her to guess he'd been spying on her. At the moment she looked a great deal like a Gypsy, he thought, continuing into the room. Her face was cast in shadows, causing her brown eyes to appear nearly ebony. Her long tresses fell freely down around her shoulders and onto her back in a carefree, feminine array and, with a bit of imagination, her loose-fitting cotton robe could pass for a fortune-teller's gown. The effect was very appealing.

"The kitchen is down the hall to your left," she said, fighting a bout of embarrassment. She preferred to keep this part of her life very private. Most people, she knew, thought Tarot-card reading was a foolish superstition.

Eric ignored the dismissal in her voice, his attention caught by the artistry of the cards. "Those look as if they were hand drawn."

"They were," she admitted stiffly. "My great-grandmother made them for me."

Eric grinned. "So she was the Gypsy."

"She was a hardworking farmer's wife," Roxy corrected curtly. Again dismissal entered her voice. "I thought you said you were thirsty."

Again Eric ignored her unspoken demand that he go away. This was a side of his hostess he'd never expected, and his curiosity was whetted. Not wanting to offend her further, he hid his skepticism behind a mask of interest. "Are you any good at doing readings?"

Roxy expected to see cynical amusement in his eyes. It wasn't there. Still, she wasn't ready to believe he had any real respect for the reading of the cards. She judged his nature to be too conservative for that. Guessing that he was merely being polite, she said, "I don't do readings for other people. They expect the cards to tell them too much."

Eric was intrigued. She honestly believed in the cards. "But you read them for yourself. What do they tell you?"

"They warn me if my path is following a dangerous course and they give me signposts that will guide me in the right direction."

Eric's gaze had locked onto one of the turned-up cards. "What does that one represent?"

She considered lying, but instinct warned her against it. She was certain he would know. "You."

The realization of why he was there hit him full force. "You allowed me to stay because it was in the cards that I should?"

She frowned at the array on the table. "Somehow you're to be involved in my getting Jamie back."

Eric's skepticism grew stronger. Clearly she was using the cards as a way of keeping her hopes up. "And which card represents him?"

"This one." Roxy tenderly touched a card to her right. Fear rippled through her. "Lately the cards warn of a stronger sadness and danger surrounding him. I have to get him back soon."

"You were going to turn another card over," Eric said, recalling how she'd quickly dropped the last card back on its face when he'd made his presence known.

"It was one of no consequence."

Before she could stop him, he flipped the card over. The image was that of an unclothed man and woman. Beneath was written The Lovers. "Us?" he asked, finding himself wondering what her lips would taste like.

"The cards merely suggest routes we can take. They don't determine our destinies," she said in clipped tones, and began to gather the deck together.

The ice in her voice told him that she fully intended to ignore the implications of the last card. For a moment he experienced a rush of disappointment. In the next instant he was mocking himself. He didn't need any complications in his life at the moment and Roxy Dugan would definitely be a complication.

"Good night," Roxy said firmly as she rose and reached for the switch on the lamp.

This time he did take his cue, reminding himself to head into the kitchen for the drink of water he'd claimed he wanted. As he filled the glass then took a drink, he marveled at the many-faceted Ms. Dugan.

He was aware that some very powerful people believed in the various arts of prophecy but he'd thought she had a more practical nature. A suspicion he didn't like began to nag at him.

Lying in her bed, Roxy couldn't get Eric's image out of her mind. With it came the memory of The Lovers card. "Thoughts like that are only going to lead to disappointment and embarrassment," she grumbled at herself. She'd thought she'd accepted the fact that she would have to live out the rest of her life without male companionship. Apparently her mind had, but her body hadn't. "Well, get used to it," she growled, looking down at herself. "Nobody wants something as mangled and useless as you."

Her jaw forming a hard line, she ordered herself to sleep.

The next morning Eric was sitting at the kitchen table drinking his second cup of coffee when Roxy entered. He'd woken early and already eaten. As she began to scramble her eggs, he studied her. Dressed in slacks and a plain white blouse with her hair pulled back and tightly braided, she moved with rigid efficiency. There was no evidence in her appearance or her manner reminiscent of the Gypsy-like creature he'd glimpsed last night. A part of him was disappointed.

Abruptly she turned to him. "I wish you'd quit staring at me. Just because I read Tarot cards doesn't mean I'm a kook." She grimaced self-consciously. "Eccentric maybe, but not daft or crazy."

"To be honest, I'm not certain what you are," he said bluntly. "We've barely spoken since my first day here."

"I'll admit, I'm a private person." The way he continued to study her as if she had an eye in the middle of her forehead caused a rush of fear. What if he decided to leave? The cards seemed insistent that his presence was necessary for her to get Jamie back. "I've had a few hard knocks in my life. They've made me very cautious about people."

"I don't like being used." Eric stated openly the suspicion that had been nagging at him ever since last night. "If you've involved me in some plan or scheme, you'd better tell me about it now."

She met his gaze levelly. "There is no scheme or plan. I don't even know why your presence here should matter. In fact, it's started causing gossip."

Eric raised an eyebrow questioningly.

"I've told everyone that you're merely helping me repair the house, but I've noticed a few skewed glances," she elaborated. "The truth is, I've considered asking you to leave. I don't want my reputation questioned. That could cause trouble. But in the past I've ignored the cards and lived to regret it."

Her frustration obviously was genuine. The depth of her belief in the cards was again also evident. Eric didn't like encouraging that, but he hated seeing her so upset. "Maybe my helping you get this place in shape is why I'm here. They say timing is everything. It could be that you were running out of time for the repairs."

Roxy shrugged. "Maybe." Her chin trembled. "Or maybe I'm looking for things in the cards that aren't there."

At least she wasn't totally impractical where the cards were concerned, he thought with relief. But, although she'd opened the door for him to voice his own skepticism, the anguish in her eyes made him want to comfort her. "I'm not convinced anyone can read the future, but I do believe in instincts," he said. "With me, it's a prickling sensation on the back of the neck that warns me when I'm headed for trouble. What do your instincts tell you?"

They tell me that having you here could cause me a great deal of frustration and grief, her inner voice responded, admitting that in spite of the harsh talk she'd had with herself the night before, she continued to be attracted to him. A part of her wanted desperately to believe that she'd misread the cards and it was safe to send him on his way. But she knew that part was allowing itself to be guided by fear. After a moment's hesitation, she said aloud, "They tell me to believe in the cards."

He wasn't certain he'd done her a favor by reestablishing her belief in the Tarot, but the relief he saw in her eyes brought pleasure and he smiled crookedly. "Then that's what I'd suggest you do," he heard himself saying.

His smile was infectious and she started to smile back. *Careful,* her inner voice warned. *He's getting very close to breaking down the wall of protection you've built.* Her jaw tensed, stopping the smile, and she turned back to the stove.

Eric frowned at her back. He could almost see the icy barrier she was determined to keep between them, and he experienced a rush of frustration. *You don't really want to get involved with a woman who lets a deck of cards guide her life, do you?* he chided himself. The frustration lessened and he rose. "I've got a lot of work to do," he said, carrying his cup to the sink and rinsing it out. "Have a good day," he added, and left.

Alone in the kitchen, Roxy looked down at her overly cooked eggs. "How do nuns do it?" she muttered. Maybe she'd stop in at the video store and get a tape on yoga or meditation or maybe one of each. "Or I could just picture the expression of horror on his face that will appear if he ever sees me disrobed." This thought brought a cold chill and her barrier once again grew strong.

A few minutes later Eric watched from the ladder as Roxy drove away. He didn't understand why the urge to help her was actually growing stronger. She wouldn't even allow him to be a friend. He concluded that Maude and the boy Jamie were behind his increasing desire to help. The boy's story reminded him of his own youth. As for Maude, she'd liked Roxy enough to leave her this place. That meant Maude would have wanted him to help, and he owed Maude.

Returning his attention to the window frame he was caulking, he considered the Tarot cards. Although he was skeptical about them, he couldn't make himself entirely discount the fact that some people had a sixth sense. The cards could simply be Roxy's way of communicating with her inner voice.

As he'd told her, with him it was a prickling on the back of his neck. A couple of times the effect had been so intense he'd known that when he turned around he'd be facing the criminal he was after. Sometimes it had taken a while to collect the evidence before he could arrest the man or woman, but at least he'd known who to keep an eye on and who never to turn his back on again.

He grimaced self-mockingly. The problem was knowing how to interpret that prickling. He'd felt it when he'd dated Susan Irving, but he'd believed it was because he thought she wanted a commitment.

"And it could be that Roxy's instincts aren't working properly this time and she's interpreting the cards incorrectly," he muttered under his breath. Besides, he admitted, as open-minded as he tried to be, he still couldn't make himself believe that a deck of cards could tell anyone anything. It was too much like looking into a crystal ball or using some other conjurer's trick.

And maybe he was trying to help the wrong person. He'd always been a sucker for a maiden in distress, but just maybe the attachment between Roxy and the boy was more one-sided than she'd led him to believe and Jamie might be happier without her. Maude had a soft heart and preferred to see the good in everyone. She could have overlooked or missed the faults that had caused the social services people to take Jamie away from Roxy. On the other hand, it had been Eric's experience that the social services people sometimes made mistakes.

And consulting his instincts didn't help. Roxy Dugan caused a confusing mix.

"I'll just bide my time for a few more days and see what develops," he decided.

Chapter Four

Three days later Eric was sitting on the front porch taking an afternoon break when an ancient-looking pickup truck came down the long dirt drive. It stopped in front of the house and an old man and a young boy climbed out. Eric judged the man to be a farmer by his manner, his bib overalls and his leathery-looking skin that gave evidence of him having spent a great deal of time in the weather. The boy was somewhere around nine or ten years old, Eric decided, and slender to the point of looking unhealthy. His long, shaggy black hair needed a cut and a good combing and his clothes, clearly hand-me-downs, were dirty and didn't fit properly. Slung on his back was a heavily laden knapsack.

"Afternoon," Eric said, rising and climbing down from the porch.

The old man continued toward him and extended a hand. "Afternoon. You the handyman who's been helping Roxy get this place in shape?"

"Yes." Accepting the handshake, Eric noticed that the

boy had stopped several feet back and was standing immobile staring at him with an unnerving intensity. He cast a smile toward the youth, but the child's gaze remained coolly distant. *Remind you of someone else you know?* he mused dryly. He'd been thinking of Roxy. Suddenly he was thinking of himself and recalling that his manner and expression hadn't been much different from that of the child's when he'd been dropped off at Maude's door.

"Found the boy a few miles down the road. Recognized him as one of Maude and Roxy's. I told him the place was closed, but appears he's determined to come back. Don't talk much. Not at all, actually."

Eric's gaze jerked to the boy. *Jamie?* he wondered, recalling Roxy's determined belief the boy would return to the farm. But even she, he was certain, wasn't expecting this kind of arrival.

"Figured Roxy'd know best what to do with him," the farmer concluded, and with a small salute of goodbye he turned back to his truck. Pausing by the youth, he shook his head. "You best start putting some meat on those bones. A strong gust of wind could blow you away."

The boy made no response. Not even acknowledging the farmer's presence, he continued to stand rigid, staring at Eric.

"Strange one, that one," the farmer muttered.

"Thanks for dropping him off," Eric called out, suddenly realizing he should say something.

The farmer cast back a glance that indicated that he wasn't so certain he'd done Eric a favor, then he climbed into his truck and left.

Eric barely noticed his departure. His attention had returned to the boy. If he was right about the child's identity, then Roxy's attachment hadn't been one-sided.

"Roxy's in town working," he said. "How about if I fix you something to eat while you wait?"

The boy nodded and headed toward the house. Eric followed him inside. As the child continued up to the second floor, obviously with a destination in mind, Eric went into the kitchen.

A few minutes later the boy joined him. He'd washed his face and hands and made an attempt to smooth his tangled mass of hair. Maude had always insisted the boys come to the table with clean hands and face, Eric recalled.

There had been fried chicken left from the night before and he'd put the platter on the table along with a glass of milk and a loaf of bread. The boy ate hungrily. Standing, leaning on the counter watching him, Eric wondered when he'd last had a meal.

"There's some ice cream if you have room for dessert," he offered when the boy finished a third piece of chicken and didn't reach for a fourth.

The boy nodded.

In an experiment to see if he could make the boy speak, Eric asked, "Vanilla or chocolate or both?"

For a long moment the boy made no response, then he held up two fingers.

Eric was now certain of the identity of this newcomer. He dished up two bowls of ice cream and seated himself at the table. "I'm Eric," he introduced himself.

The boy looked up momentarily from his bowl of ice cream in acknowledgment but said nothing before returning his attention to the sweet treat.

"Can I assume you're Jamie?" Eric asked bluntly.

The boy merely looked up at the clock on the wall. It read three-fifteen.

Taking a guess that the child was wondering when Roxy would be home, Eric said, "Roxy's on the seven-to-three shift. She was going to do a little shopping when she finished work. I'm expecting her back around four.''

Quickly finishing his ice cream, the youth carried his bowl, plate and glass to the sink, washed them and put them in the dish drainer. Then he put the chicken and bread away and left the kitchen.

Eric washed his own bowl, then went looking for the boy. He found him sitting on the front porch step, his gaze locked on the road.

"I was caulking windows," Eric said. "If you need me, just yell or make some sort of noise."

The boy gave no sign that he'd even heard.

"Make yourself at home," Eric added, and went back to work. Old memories flashed through his mind as he climbed the ladder. He'd sat in that same place, with that same intense expression on his face, for days after his grandparents had brought him here. As lousy as life with them had been, accepting the fact that they'd dumped him off like a bag of garbage had been difficult. He'd imagined them coming back in tears, telling him that they'd realized they loved him and wanted him back. But they hadn't come, and eventually he'd accepted the fact that as far as his family was concerned, he was disposed of, never to be thought of again.

The sound of a car's engine caught his attention. He looked toward the main road and saw Roxy turning onto the long drive. Climbing down from the ladder, he walked to the corner of the house and stopped. From there he could observe her and the boy.

Nearing the house, Roxy blinked, certain she was seeing things. Then the tears began to flow. Parking the car with a screech, she jumped out and hurried toward the porch. A few feet from Jamie, she came to an abrupt halt. He had risen, but his expression wasn't one of happy greeting. His back was straight with defiant pride and he was looking at her with hurtful accusation.

"I didn't come to visit like I promised because they wouldn't tell me where you were," she said, brushing at her tears. "I've been working, getting the house into shape, hoping they would let me have you back." She saw his bottom lip tremble and then go crooked and knew he was biting on the inside to keep it firm. "I missed you," she said, holding her arms out toward him.

Suddenly he was running into her embrace.

Watching them, Eric couldn't deny the bond between them, and he envied Jamie. He'd never had that kind of love. Maude had loved him, but she'd loved all of her boys the same. She'd been more of a kindly aunt than a mother. The relationship between Jamie and Roxy clearly went much deeper.

Holding the boy close, Roxy felt panic sweep through her. He was much too thin. Loosing her hold, she gently grasped him by the upper arms and moved him a little away from her for a more thorough inspection. "Didn't they feed you? And those clothes. Surely the social services people provided money for you to have clothes."

He shrugged as if to say those things didn't matter.

Continuing to kneel in front of him, she combed his hair away from his face with her fingers. "How did you get here?"

From the pocket of the baggy pants, he pulled out a map and proudly displayed it.

"You found your way here on your own?" she demanded, and the hope that he'd been legitimately returned to her vanished. "You ran away?"

Again he shrugged as if that didn't matter.

"Where did you run away from?"

He pointed to Philadelphia.

Horror at what could have happened to him along the way caused her stomach to knot. "That's over thirty miles."

He frowned as if her concern was childish.

Tears of joy and relief again flowed as she drew him back into her arms.

"Looks like we've got company coming," Eric said, moving toward them.

Roxy recognized the car. Her hold on Jamie tightened. "It's Mary Chambers from social services."

Two pairs of accusing eyes turned on Eric.

He scowled. "I didn't tell anyone he was here, but it stands to reason that the authorities would check to see if he'd made contact. Or maybe the farmer who picked him up felt it was his civic duty to report him."

"Go inside," Roxy ordered the boy, and he quickly obeyed.

"Looks like Jamie found his way back," Mary noted, getting out of her car and approaching Eric and Roxy.

Keeping his expression friendly, Eric made a quick appraisal, sizing her up for battle. She was medium in build with graying hair and had the manner of someone there on official business, but there was a softness in her eyes that suggested that she was not an enemy.

Roxy stepped in front of the woman, barring her from continuing to the house. "He looks as if he hasn't eaten in weeks and his clothes are a disgrace. You assured me he was being well looked after." A bitter edge entered her voice. "Better than I could look after him." She repeated the social worker's words.

Mary's official manner softened and apology showed on her face. "We had to send him back to Philadelphia. That's where his family was. They tried to reunite them, but no one would take him in, so he went into the system there.''

Roxy knew Mary had a good heart. "You want to see what happened to him?" She glanced over her shoulder toward the house. "Jamie, come out."

Reluctantly, the boy obeyed.

Eric watched the social worker's face. Her jaw stiffened, but she didn't appear surprised.

"They told me he'd begun to refuse to eat," she said. "I checked his record. He's been in five different homes since he left here. In spite of the counseling provided, he continued to refuse to speak. After a short while in each home, the foster parents would call social services and say they felt they couldn't help him and request that he be moved."

Jamie had come to stand beside Roxy. Eric glanced at him and noticed that he was holding her hand so tightly both were white.

Mary's gaze continued to rest on the child's gaunt features. "I really thought he'd be better off in a real home."

Roxy scowled. "This is a real home."

Mary frowned back. "You have to work. When school isn't in session, he'd be on his own all day. And boys need a father figure."

"I'd have found someone to watch over him," Roxy shot back. "And a lot of kids grow up in single-parent homes and turn out just fine as long as they're loved and wanted, and he is loved and wanted here."

Mary breathed a harsh sigh. "There's nothing I can do. He's not in my jurisdiction. He's part of the Philadelphia system and they want him back."

Roxy shifted so that Jamie was behind her. "They can't have him back. They've done enough damage."

Mary scowled. "The law is on their side."

"If you send him back and he again refuses to eat, he could die," Eric cautioned, deciding it was time for him to step into the fray. "He doesn't look as if he's got much more weight to lose before he's in serious trouble."

For a long moment Mary said nothing, her gaze resting on the boy. Abruptly her attention shifted to Roxy. "Do you still have that paper his grandmother signed giving Maude guardianship?"

Hope blossomed in Roxy. "Yes."

"I'll take it to Judge Blaire. He's an old friend and supporter of Maude's. I'll argue that since she left you everything, the guardianship should revert to you."

"I tried that," Roxy reminded her icily, recalling that, at that time, Mary had argued against her.

"This time I'll be on your side." Mary's shoulders straightened defensively. "He and I were merely trying to do what we thought was best for the boy."

Roxy ordered herself not to be so hostile. She needed this woman's aid. "And you think that he'll reconsider and grant me guardianship?"

"I don't know if he'll go that far, but if I can get you temporary custody, that will give you time to pursue a legal guardianship."

Roxy nodded her consent.

Mary's gaze again turned to the boy. "Until I get a ruling from the judge, he can stay here. I'll call Philadelphia and tell them I've placed him in a home here until a decision can be reached. I doubt they'll fight me on this. In spite of what you probably think, we all want what's best for him."

"You don't want to know what I think," Roxy said.

Mary's gaze again rested on the child's gaunt features. "I can't blame you for questioning the system," she admitted, then turned her attention back to Roxy. "If you'll get me that paper, I'll be on my way."

It was curious, Eric thought as he sat eating dinner. No one was talking and yet there was a comfortable atmosphere in the room, as if the world was in balance. In spite of the worry in Roxy's eyes, there was a glow about her. Jamie was eating again as if trying to make up for all the meals he'd skipped. As for himself, Eric didn't know how he fit in, but he felt a curious kinship to the other two that was unique to anything he'd experienced before.

Now that she was actually sitting at the same table with Jamie again, Roxy admitted to herself that she'd been terrified she might never see him again. Covertly she glanced at Eric. Where did he fit into the scheme of things? Every instinct told her that his presence was necessary to make everything right. The Lovers' card again entered her mind. Her jaw tightened. That was not part of the solution!

Jamie yawned widely and blinked his eyes as if having trouble staying awake.

Roxy smiled with motherly warmth. "Go take a bath. I'll make up your bed."

He nodded and left, with Roxy close behind.

Eric was finishing a piece of apple pie when she returned. "Nice kid," he said, rising and helping her clear the table.

Her expression remaining grim, she nodded and glanced toward the phone. That Mary Chambers hadn't called yet had his nerves on edge, too, he admitted, and allowed silence to hang between them while they finished cleaning up the kitchen. When the job was finished, Roxy went upstairs to check on Jamie. A few minutes later she came looking for Eric.

Following their usual routine, he'd gone back to working on the house.

Motioning for him to come down from the ladder, she said, "Jamie's sleeping. I don't want to disturb him, so we'll skip working on the house this evening. Besides, I don't want to miss Mary's call."

Eric nodded. A little later, after cleaning up, he went into the living room to watch the news on television. Roxy was there, standing staring at the phone, her arms wrapped around herself as if she was physically trying to hold herself under control.

"With the social worker on your side and the judge being a friend of Maude's, I'm sure he'll grant you custody," he said, attempting to ease her strain.

Roxy's hold on herself tightened even more. "I've learned never to count on anything."

Again Eric found himself wondering what had happened to cause her to be so disillusioned with the world. She had family who obviously cared for her and whom she cared for. He'd heard that in her voice when they'd called.

Continuing to stare at the phone, Roxy tried to think only positive thoughts, but she couldn't keep the fear that the news would be bad from creeping into her mind. "I won't let them take him away from me," she vowed.

Again Eric felt the need to say something encouraging. "I'm sure everything will work out for the best."

Her gaze swung to him. "You can't be sure of that! No one can be certain of anything in this life. One minute everything can be going along just fine, then suddenly a person's whole world can come crashing down and everything you thought was real and true is nothing but ashes." Roxy clamped her mouth shut. She was letting her anxiety cause her to talk too much.

"That's what happened to you? Your whole world came crashing down?" Eric prodded.

"Something like that," she muttered, furious that she'd blurted out so much.

Eric knew she didn't want to talk further, but he didn't like being in the dark. If he was to be instrumental in her keeping Jamie, he wanted to know what was motivating her. "And Jamie is your phoenix risen from the ashes? That's a pretty tall order for a young child."

She drew a shaky breath. "Jamie is Jamie. He needs me."

Eric continued to study her narrowly. "I think it'd be fairer to say that both of you need each other. The question is, is your need so selfish that it will bring harm to the boy in the end?"

Roxy saw the skepticism in his eyes and knew he was wondering if he should be helping her. The cards had been right so far. He'd come and Jamie had returned. Eric couldn't leave yet. His part, whatever that part was, hadn't been played out. Her instincts told her that. They also told her that she was going to have to tell the truth. "I will never knowingly cause Jamie any pain, but you're right. I need him, too. I was six months pregnant when I was in a commuter train accident. I lost my child and the ability to have any more. I was devastated. As if that wasn't enough, Tom, my *loving husband,* couldn't live with the idea of not having children he'd sired, so he divorced me." Pride flashed in her eyes. "I took back my maiden name and put him out of my mind."

"And then came to work for Maude to fill the void in your life," Eric prodded when she fell silent.

"Actually, coming here wasn't my idea. It was my grandmother's. She knew Maude could use some help."

Eric saw the shadow of uneasiness cross Roxy's features and was certain she was leaving something out. The cards again? he wondered. "And I suppose you consulted your Tarot deck and it told you to come."

She didn't want him to think she was a kook who let the cards make her decisions for her. "It was the nightmares that convinced me to come here. About a year after I lost my baby, I began to wake in a cold sweat from a recurring dream in which a child was crying for help. When my grandmother suggested I come here, I reasoned that working with children who needed love might be the solution. Besides, I needed something to do that made me feel really useful. I hadn't gone to college. The only thing I'd wanted in life was to be a wife and mother. I married Tom right out of high school and worked as a cashier and waitress to put him through college and graduate school. Then we'd started trying for a family." The harsh pain of betrayal swept through her and she clamped her mouth shut. Again she was letting her nerves cause her to rattle on about a part of her life she wanted to forget.

"And did the dreams stop?" Eric asked when her pause lengthened into a silence.

"They stopped when Jamie came. They started again when he was taken away." She met his gaze with defiance. "I know you probably don't think the kind of bond I'm describing can happen between a woman and child who aren't biologically related, but it's there. He's as much a son to me as any child I could have borne."

Eric wasn't convinced that the dreams were proof of a special bond between Jamie and Roxy. It seemed more reasonable that their original occurrence was due to Roxy's deep mourning for the child she'd lost. When Jamie was taken away they returned because again she'd lost a child she'd learned to love. But whatever the reason, he was convinced that Roxy cared for the boy as much as any mother could care for a son.

The ringing of the phone caused Roxy to jump slightly. Grabbing up the receiver, she managed to issue a stiff "Hello."

"Roxy, it's Mary." Mary Chambers's voice came over the line. "I've convinced Judge Blaire to give you temporary custody, but he suggests that you seek a permanent resolution as soon as possible."

Mary's first words had brought a surge of relief, but the hesitant edge in her voice toward the end caused that relief to vanish. "A permanent resolution?"

"Legally the judge doesn't have jurisdiction over the boy. If the Philadelphia authorities challenge his ruling, it will, most likely, be overturned. The only way you can be assured of keeping Jamie would be to adopt him."

Roxy fought back a rush of panic. "You don't sound as if you think that's possible."

"I've checked his file. All of the living grandparents signed releases that allow the boy to be adopted. But you'll have to meet the requirements for an adoptive parent."

Roxy's jaw firmed. "I'll do whatever is necessary."

"Then come by my office tomorrow and I'll outline the procedure."

"I can be there at three-thirty," Roxy replied, ignoring the doubt in the other woman's voice.

"What's going on?" Eric asked as she hung up.

"I have temporary custody, but to keep him I'm going to have to adopt him, and that's exactly what I'm going to do." Her jaw set in a determined line, she strode out of the room.

Eric frowned thoughtfully as she disappeared from view. He was under the impression that being married was a requirement for adoption. Of course, times change, and he had missed three years of societal evolution. The Lovers' card again came to mind and he frowned. He had a strong feeling that for Ms. Dugan, lovemaking and marriage were synonymous. Was she expecting him to marry her in order to provide the needed husband? If she was, she was going to have to think twice. He wasn't looking for any ties that bind. In the next moment he was mocking himself. The lady had made it perfectly clear that she had no intention of pursuing any relationship of a personal nature with him. If she did go looking for a mate, he wouldn't be on her list.

Lying in bed later, Roxy tried to hold on to positive thoughts, but the worry that she would not be able to meet the requirements plagued her. A husband would improve her position greatly. Eric's image came into her mind, and again desire began to slowly simmer within her. *No!* her inner voice said sternly. She would not face masculine rejection again. She would do this on her own.

Chapter Five

The next morning Eric was on the ladder painting the upper level while Jamie was on the ground several feet away painting the lower when a car Eric didn't recognize came down the drive. Climbing down, he went to meet the new arrival. A man in a suit, a little on the plump side, bald on the dome of his head with a fringe of white hair around the sides and back, climbed out of the vehicle. Eric guessed his age to be in the mid- to late sixties.

"I'm Judge Raymond Blaire," the newcomer introduced himself, extending a hand.

"Eric Bishop," Eric replied, accepting the handshake. Noticing Jamie had come to stand beside him, he added, "And this is Jamie."

Releasing Eric, the judge eyed the boy with a friendly expression. "So you found your way back. Can't say I blame you. There was always a lot of love in this house."

Jamie simply stared at the man, his expression guarded.

"Guess if I'd been through what you've been through, I wouldn't be too trusting, either," Judge Blaire said. His tone became one of fatherly command. "Looks like you've got a big painting job ahead of you. Why don't you run along and get back to it? I need to speak to Mr. Bishop alone."

For a moment the boy hesitated, then at a quick trot he disappeared around the side of the house.

"Unusual child," the judge commented.

"A special child," Eric corrected, surprised by the strength of his need to defend Jamie.

"Yes, of course. Special," the judge replied impatiently. His expression hardened as his gaze leveled on Eric. "I didn't come here to play a game of semantics. I'm a plainspoken man who says what he thinks. The boy's different. Knowing his history I can understand why, but that doesn't change the reality. Roxy's the only one who's been able to get through to him. She's a strange one herself, but Maude thought highly of her and I respect Maude's judgment."

The judge's description of Roxy as "strange" irked Eric. "Roxy's been through a lot herself," he said frostily.

The judge frowned as if angry with himself for speaking so openly. "I didn't mean any offense."

Feeling the need to say more in Roxy's defense, Eric added, "She's a strong woman and has a lot of love to give the boy. If you ask me, he couldn't find anyone who would be a more devoted mother."

The judge nodded. "I agree, and I'd like to see her be able to keep him."

Eric heard the doubt in the man's voice. "You think she'll run into trouble when she tries to adopt him?"

"Nothing has changed much since they told her she didn't meet the requirements." Judge Blaire's gaze became harder. "Except maybe her reputation isn't as untarnished as it used to be."

The implication in the man's words was clear. "There's nothing going on between Roxy and me," Eric assured him. "I'm just helping to get the house into better shape."

"Too bad."

Surprised by this reaction, Eric raised an eyebrow questioningly.

"If she had a husband and that husband had a steady job, it'd help get rid of a lot of the roadblocks. Rumor has it that you're a military man and just here recuperating from an injury."

"I do have steady work waiting for me when I leave here," Eric replied in answer to the question in the judge's voice.

Clearly wanting to be certain the point he was trying to get across was received, the older man locked his gaze onto Eric's. "Like I said, too bad there isn't anything going on between you and Roxy. I'll do what I can for her, but the government's got a lot of requirements and restrictions. Right now about the only things she has in her favor are the paper granting guardianship to Maude and my knowledge of how much Maude depended on her. Neither of those would hold much legal weight if anyone decided to challenge." He extended his hand. "Thanks for your time."

A couple of minutes later, as Eric stood watching the judge's car going down the road, he became aware that Jamie had again come to stand beside him. Looking down at the boy, he saw the questioning plea in the child's eyes and knew Jamie had been eavesdropping on his and the judge's conversation.

"I'm not the 'family man' type," he said. "Besides, I don't think Roxy considers me husband material."

Worry spread over the boy's face as his gaze shifted to the judge's car disappearing in the distance.

Again Eric experienced a strong surge of kinship toward the child. "But I'll do whatever I can to help."

The worry remaining on his face, Jamie merely nodded, then strode stiffly back around the side of the house and began to paint once again.

Eric followed. He'd never thought about having a family. He'd always thought of himself as the Lone Ranger type, saving the world from the bad guys and then riding off alone into the sunset. And that was still how he saw himself. He'd do what he could to help Roxy, but there were limits.

Driving home late that afternoon, Roxy fought threatened nausea caused by anxiousness. Mary Chambers had not been encouraging. Under some circumstances, adoption rights were granted to single parents, but only if that single parent had a much better income than the one Roxy was earning. The fact that Roxy owned the farm might help, Mary had admitted, but she hadn't sounded encouraging.

Jamie ran to meet her as she parked and climbed out of the car. "Did you have a good day?" she asked, putting an arm around his shoulders as they walked toward the house.

He nodded, then looked at her and she read the question in his eyes.

"My day wasn't so great. Mrs. Chambers pointed out some stumbling blocks we have to overcome."

Worry showed on the boy's face.

She gave his shoulders a squeeze. "I promise you I won't let anyone separate us again."

He breathed a sigh of relief and smiled trustingly.

Out of the corner of her eye Roxy saw Eric putting the lid back on the paint can. A solution that had been nagging at her all the way home grew in strength. Once inside the house, she sent Jamie upstairs to wash up so he could help her cook dinner, then went into the parlor and took out the Tarot deck. Not even taking the time to seat herself, she shuffled it quickly and dealt out the cards. The Lovers' card appeared again in the sequence.

Eric had been on his way upstairs when he heard her in the parlor. He'd paused at the door and looked in to discover her so intent on the cards, she hadn't noticed his arrival. Moving close enough to see the array, he frowned. The thought that he should turn tail and run crossed his mind. Instead he heard himself saying, "Seems that card insists on turning up."

Roxy jerked around, her gaze going from the card to him. "It doesn't always mean what most people think," she said stiffly. "It can stand for a commitment between a man and a woman. Intimacy does not have to be a part of that commitment."

In spite of having just today reminded himself that he wasn't interested in forming any permanent ties, Eric found himself again thinking that her lips looked incredibly inviting. Unable to resist testing the feel of her skin, he ran a finger along the line of her jaw. "But that would take all the fun out of it."

His touch sparked desire. "I suppose it would," she conceded huskily. In the next instant she was chiding herself. There would be no more of that kind of fun for her.

Eric saw the desire in her eyes, and the urge to satisfy the wanting there grew strong. *You could be stepping into quicksand. The woman used the word* commitment. *Don't let your hormones lead you down a path you don't want to take!* his inner voice warned. But he wasn't in the mood to listen. What he had labeled as curiosity had, he confessed, been a growing attraction. And even though that attraction was, he reasoned, due merely to his long lack of female companionship, he couldn't stop himself from acting on it. Catching her chin with the tips of his fingers, he tilted her face upward. "You have very inviting lips."

"You do, too." She flushed when she realized she'd spoken, and ordered herself to back away from him. But her legs refused to obey.

A smile of masculine triumph tilted one corner of his mouth. Leaning forward, he tasted her lips.

Roxy's heart pounded frantically. The urge to move into his arms was close to overwhelming.

His hands left her face to travel down her arms to her elbows. When she offered no resistance, he drew her closer and let his hands move to her back for a continued caressing exploration of her body.

She was beginning to feel like purring when he reached her hips. Abruptly, the cold chill of reality spread through her. "No." She backed out of his reach.

Eric frowned at the panic in her eyes. "I wasn't going to force myself on you. It was just a kiss."

Jerking her gaze away from him, she began to gather up the cards. "I need to get dinner started."

Frustration swept through Eric. He was tired of playing games. He wanted to know what made Roxy Dugan tick. Catching her by the upper arms, he forced her to face him. "What did your ex-husband do to you?"

The coldness within her became ice. "He didn't do anything." She attempted to jerk free.

Eric's hold tightened, refusing her her freedom. "He must have done something. It's obvious that you're terrified of letting a man touch you."

"No!" An animal-like shriek split the air.

Startled, both Eric and Roxy turned to the door to discover Jamie there. He was white as a sheet and trembling like a leaf in a high wind. His hands were clasped over his mouth and there was sheer terror on his face.

Releasing Roxy immediately, Eric held his hands up, palms open toward the boy. "I wasn't hurting her. I would never do that."

Roxy could barely believe her ears. Jamie had spoken! But this realization was overshadowed by the panic in his eyes. Hurrying to him, she took his hands in hers and held them with firm reassurance. "I'm fine. Really."

"I should have been quiet," he choked out. "I could have gotten you killed, just like I did my mom."

"No, you couldn't have. Eric wasn't going to hurt me," she soothed, releasing his hands and wrapping her arms around him. In sterner tones she added, "And you can't blame yourself for your mother's death."

Jamie pushed free. "You weren't there. You don't know." Tears streaming down his face, he fled up the stairs.

For a moment Roxy stood frozen. Not only was he talking, but the control he normally held over himself was gone. It was as if a dam had burst and all the pent-up emotions he'd been storing were pouring forth. In the next instant she was running after him.

Eric followed on her heels. The guilt etched into Jamie's face and the wild look in his eyes made him afraid of what the child might do to himself.

Entering the boy's room, they found him huddled on the floor in a corner, his arms wrapped around his legs, his body still trembling violently.

Kneeling in front of him, Roxy gently stroked his face. "You were only six. There was nothing you could do to stop your father."

He pulled away from her touch, wedging himself as far as was physically possible into the angle of the walls.

Eric stood behind Roxy. "I've seen men when they're in the mood to kill," he said. "It takes the threat of their own death to stop them, and sometimes even that isn't enough if their rage has taken over or if their mind is clouded by drugs or alcohol."

Jamie looked up at him. A stillness filled the room as the boy studied the man. It was a heavy silence that made breathing difficult and set every nerve in Roxy's body on edge. She was tempted to speak, to break this uncomfortable quiet, but a deeper instinct kept her silent.

Eric met the boy's gaze levelly. He'd seen a great deal of pain in his life, but never any more intense than that of this child.

"My mother told me to leave the room. To be quiet." Jamie's words came out in a harsh whisper as if speaking them was causing him great strain. "I started to obey, but my dad kept hitting her. I wanted to make him stop. I yelled at him to stop. When he didn't, I ran back and beat at him. He kicked me. I remember flying through the air and hitting the wall." The boy paused and drew a deep, shaky breath. "I don't remember a lot after that." He frowned as if trying hard to concentrate. "I do remember the sound of the gun. That was very loud. Then I saw my mother lying on the floor. There was blood and she was very still."

Roxy held his face gently in her hands. "That was a long time ago. It's over and done with."

Jamie didn't seem to hear her. He kept his gaze locked on Eric. "If I'd left the room. If I'd been quiet. She might be alive today."

"No, she wouldn't," he replied with conviction. "The die had been cast."

A sudden realization struck Roxy. "That's why you refused to talk. Your mother told you to be quiet."

Jamie's gaze broke its hold on Eric and turned to her. "I didn't want anyone else to ever get hurt because of me."

"Hiding from life is no guarantee trouble won't find you," Eric said. "Either of you," he added, letting Roxy know he thought she was doing some hiding of her own.

Ignoring his insinuation, she kept her attention on Jamie. "The only way you can cause me any harm is if you're taken away from me again," she said. "That would break my heart."

His chin trembled. "Mine, too."

Eric experienced a jab of envy and realized he was feeling left out. He'd always been on the outside, he reminded himself curtly. That was where the fates had put him and where he belonged. More important, he was comfortable there, he assured himself.

A warm glow spread through Roxy. Combing the boy's hair back with her fingers, she said coaxingly, "How about if we go down to the kitchen and get dinner started? I don't want Mrs. Chambers accusing me of not feeding you properly."

For a long moment Jamie hesitated, then he grimaced his agreement.

Eric noticed that during the preparation of the meal and while they ate, the child reverted back to his habit of using body language to communicate. As they ate dessert, it occurred to him that if the cards were right and he did have a mission here, maybe it was simply to get the boy to talk. After all, if he hadn't made Jamie think that Roxy was in danger, there was no telling how long the child would have remained mute. "If you want to stay with Roxy, it would help her case if you began to communicate with words. I'm sure the judge and Mrs. Chambers would attribute that to her and be impressed."

Jamie studied him, clearly weighing this assessment.

Roxy felt dizzy and realized she was holding her breath waiting for a response. "It would help," she said encouragingly.

The boy's attention remained on Eric and his expression changed to one of challenge. "Swear to me that you will never hurt Roxy."

"I swear," Eric replied solemnly.

The boy remained silent for a long moment, then asked, "Do you like her?"

Eric wondered if Jamie was simply trying to reassure himself and ease his fears or if this was leading somewhere else. "Sure, I like her."

Roxy wanted to be indifferent to Eric's answer, but she couldn't stop herself from wondering just how much he liked her.

"Then you could marry her," Jamie said.

Roxy flushed scarlet. "Whatever put that notion into your head?"

He clamped his mouth shut, the tone of her voice obviously causing him to resort back to his reticent ways.

"Judge Blaire," Eric answered for the boy. "He was here today and said that if you were married to a man with a steady income, your chances for adopting would be greatly increased."

Roxy knew the judge was only trying to help, but that didn't make her embarrassment any less. She recalled the kiss in the parlor, and it occurred to her that perhaps Eric wasn't totally opposed to the idea of pursuing the judge's suggestion. She cast him a glance. He was getting handsomer with each passing day and she was willing to bet that in the past he'd had no trouble finding women to spend time with. Again the embers of desire sparked to life. On the other hand, he could have been merely looking for a romp in the hay, her practical side cautioned. Either way he'd quickly lose interest in her if he got a full look at the goods he'd be getting. "I never thought of Judge Blaire as a matchmaker," she said, then rising from the table, put an end to the conversation by beginning to clear the dishes.

Eric experienced a sharp sting of insult. Clearly, she found the judge's suggestion absurd. He'd never thought of himself as a vain man, but he wasn't used to being so blatantly rejected, and his ego was tweaked. He soothed it by reminding himself that he wasn't looking to get involved with her in the first place.

Her own turmoil now under control, Roxy's concern turned to Jamie. Rounding the table, she placed an arm around his shoulders. "I didn't mean to snap at you," she apologized. "I was just a little surprised by your suggestion." A plea entered her voice. "Eric is right. If you would begin to be a little more verbal, Mary might be able to use that as proof that staying with me is good for you."

Jamie nodded.

Roxy was disappointed by his continued silence, but she told herself that old habits aren't changed in a day.

A couple of hours later Roxy peeked into Jamie's room to assure herself that he was asleep. Still tired from the long trek that had brought him there, coupled with a day of painting and the emotional trauma of reliving his mother's death, the boy had been exhausted by the time they'd finished dinner. When she'd suggested he go directly to bed, he'd obeyed without protest.

Left alone with Eric, she hadn't been able to keep her

eyes or her thoughts off him. He'd probably left a whole string of broken hearts in his wake, she'd told herself, thinking that she'd never seen a man look so virile. Needing time on her own, she'd shooed him out of the kitchen and finished cleaning the dishes on her own. Afterward, she'd checked on Jamie to see that he was comfortably tucked in, then gone out on the back porch and sat and rocked for a long time while holding a terse argument with herself.

Now having reached a decision, and having assured herself that Jamie was still sleeping soundly, she made her way to the living room.

"The fact that Jamie actually bid us both good-night is encouraging," she said as she entered. Inwardly she frowned at herself. She'd wanted to sound as if she was making casual conversation. Instead the statement had come out stiffly.

Eric laid aside the book he'd been reading and looked at her. She was nervous, uncertain...this was not a side of her he'd seen exposed so openly before. Then her jaw firmed and he recognized the in-control woman he'd been living with. "Yes, it is," he agreed.

Too tense to sit, Roxy positioned herself behind her favorite chair. Her legs were shaky. She rested her hands on the chair's back for support. "When I met with Mary this afternoon, she told me the same thing the judge told you. It's not impossible to hope that something can be worked out if I remain single, but my chances of keeping Jamie are slim. My job would barely allow me to make ends meet, and the courts apparently seem to feel that material considerations outweigh the emotional. I know they're trying to do what's best for the child, but in some instances, they're wrong. Jamie and I could make it on our own."

Eric didn't think he'd ever seen a woman with more purpose in her eyes. "I'm sure you could."

Roxy drew a deep breath, hoping to calm her increasing nervousness. It didn't work. The planned script she'd rehearsed fled from her mind. "However, since you and I are the only ones who seem certain of that, I was wondering if you'd consider marrying me." Her words echoed in her ears. Spoken aloud they sounded like lunacy, but there was no taking them back. "It wouldn't be forever. Just until I get Jamie," she added hurriedly.

The stunned expression on his face caused nausea to bubble in her throat. He wasn't going to agree. She'd approached this all wrong and made a complete fool of herself. "You probably aren't interested. Forget I asked," she blurted, and strode out of the room.

Continuing through the house, she exited the back door and stood on the porch, leaning on the railing, gasping in air. "You certainly handled that well," she mocked herself under her breath. She'd planned to ask him how he felt about being a Good Samaritan, and if his response had been hesitant or he'd hedged, she was going to stop right there. If it was positive, she was going to work her way slowly to the proposal. Instead, she'd let her nerves take control.

Eric sat staring at the doorway through which Roxy had fled. Her proposal had been a momentary surprise, then he'd reminded himself of how deeply she cared for Jamie. What did continue to surprise him was his attitude. She was wrong. He was interested. "Well, I did promise Jamie I'd do what I could." But it wasn't Jamie he was thinking of as he rose and followed the path she'd taken. What he was thinking of was her in his bed. *Don't you think marrying a woman simply to bed her is a little extreme?* his inner voice argued.

She needs a husband and I might as well be him, he rebutted, ending the mental debate.

Hearing the back screen door opening, Roxy straightened, squaring her shoulders.

"I told you I would help," Eric said, halting a few feet from her. "If you need a husband for a while, I can handle that."

There was a husky edge in his voice that caused Roxy's blood to race. The taste of his lips came back to taunt her and a fire ignited within. *Get real!* she mocked herself dryly, and the fire went out. She turned to face him. "It would be a marriage in name only."

"That could be very frustrating." Moving closer, he traced the line of her jaw with his fingertip. "Besides, a man should get some sort of reward for doing a good deed."

She ordered her body to be immune to his touch. It refused to cooperate. Her blood heated and the fires of passion began to smolder.

Eric saw the beginning glow of desire in her eyes. "All work and no play is no way to live." He kissed the tip of her nose, then lightly tasted her lips. "We might as well enjoy ourselves."

Intending to push him away, she brought her hands up to press against his chest. But instead of showing resistance, they rested there, palms flat, the sturdy feel of him causing the embers within to flare into flame. She imagined how he would look unclothed and the fire threatened to consume her.

Sensing victory, Eric began a slow, caressing exploration. His hands moved to her neck, then over her shoulders, and began a slow descent down her back. He couldn't remember when a woman had felt so good beneath his touch. But then, it had been a long time since he'd been with a woman, he reminded himself.

Roxy had been certain her ex-husband's behavior had humiliated her so greatly that no man would ever be able to reawaken her passionate side so intensely again. She'd been wrong. Her body ached for the kind of fulfillment Eric's caress suggested he could provide. Shock waves of warning suddenly flashed in her mind. His exploration had reached her hips. In her mind's eye she saw her ex-husband's face. She could not subject herself to that kind of rejection again! Frantically, she struggled to break free.

Frustration raged through Eric. He wanted her and he knew she'd wanted him, but something was making her afraid. Freeing her, he stepped back and took a long, calming breath. Getting his body back under control wasn't easy. He was in need of a woman. Mentally he frowned at himself. His ability to restrain himself was usually strong, but he knew that if he agreed to this marriage, keeping his hands off her was going to be impossible. Clearly he'd been celibate far too long. "I'm willing to go along with this short-term marriage, but I'm a healthy male. I can only take so many cold showers."

He'd made his position clear. If she wanted his cooperation she was going to have to tell him the truth. Her chin threatened to tremble. She stiffened it. "I'm just trying to save us both from an embarrassing situation. No man would want this body."

Startled by her pronouncement, he frowned. She'd never struck him as the type who would be that intensely self-conscious about her body. "That's a pretty strong statement." His gaze raked over her, resting momentarily on the side that was the source of her limp, then returning to her face. "So you've got a few scars from the accident.

So what? They probably look a lot worse to you than they do to others."

"You're wrong." She met his gaze with proud defiance. "I was burned in the accident that took my baby's life. I also needed extensive surgery on my hip and there was the abdominal surgery, as well. When I finally came home from the hospital, my ex-husband couldn't even bring himself to touch me." A bitterness entered her voice. "He claimed he was worried he would hurt me. When I assured him that he wouldn't, I saw the revulsion in his eyes. I won't suffer that kind of humiliation...degradation again!" Feeling her control slipping and fearing that the hot tears behind her eyes would escape, she squared her shoulders with pride and strode past him, into the house.

Eric frowned at her departing back. "Well, now I know what's eating at the lady," he murmured as the door swung closed behind her.

The hurt he'd seen in her eyes tore at him. He wanted to make it go away. He also knew he was going to have to take her up on her proposal. Leaving her and Jamie to fight the system on their own wasn't his style.

Going back inside, he locked up and turned off the lights, then headed upstairs. The shower at her end of the hall was running. In his mind's eye he visualized her in there with the water cascading over her. The taste of her still lingered on his lips and his arousal returned. He added scarring, but that didn't cool the heat building within him.

Pausing at the bathroom door, he tried the knob. It was unlocked. Opening it, he entered, strode to the shower and pushed back the curtain far enough to give himself a full view. She'd been honest. There was extensive scarring over portions of her lower abdomen.

Roxy had been rinsing the soap off when the shower

curtain was pushed back. A gasp escaped, then seeing Eric looking at her disfigurement, she froze, unable to move.

"That must have hurt like hell," he said after a moment.

"It did." Recovering from her shock, she tried to cover herself with her hands and arms.

Eric's gaze traveled upward, noting the fullness of her breasts and smoothness of her shoulders before reaching her face. The scarring had done nothing to dampen his lust and he let her see that in his eyes. "I promised both you and Jamie I'd help in any way I could, and I always keep my word. I'll marry you, but on my terms. You and I will share a bed." Before Roxy could respond, he closed the curtain and left.

For a full minute, maybe more, she stood immobile. Then she began to tremble and a nervous smile played at the corners of her mouth. He'd made her feel desirable. She hadn't felt that way in so long, she didn't know whether to laugh or cry. She wanted to do both.

Don't get so excited, her inner voice cautioned. The man had been without a woman for years. He probably figured he could ignore her lesser attributes for the duration of their union. Well, she didn't care. She'd missed male companionship, too.

A nervous smile playing at the corners of her mouth, she finished her shower. Exiting the bathroom, she discovered Eric leaning on the wall opposite the door waiting for her.

"I figured we'd get the license tomorrow and get married as soon as possible after that," he said.

She shrugged what she hoped was a nonchalant shrug. "Sure. I suppose the sooner the better."

His gaze flickered over her and the blue of his eyes darkened with desire. "Definitely the sooner the better."

Roxy's blood began to race and she was tempted to invite him into her bed immediately. *But what if he's disappointed and decides to call off the wedding?* her cautious side demanded. She needed that marriage license. "Good night," she said stiffly, and hurried on to her room.

Eric frowned at her departing back. He'd seen her momentary hesitation, then her jaw firm with decision. She'd obviously decided there would be no intimacy until after the wedding. Impatience curled through him. It was never smart to want a woman so strongly, he admonished himself, and headed into the bathroom for a cold shower.

Chapter Six

The following evening Roxy sat frowning at the cards she'd laid out in front of her. With the judge's help, they were being allowed to waive the usual three-day waiting period following their application for the license. Tomorrow afternoon at one, she and Eric were to be wed in the judge's chambers. She'd called her family and told them about the wedding. Her father, mother and grandmother were coming.

Eric had called no one, and that fact had been nagging at her all day. Finally, deciding she would read the cards specifically for him, she'd put the box on the coffee table in the living room just before dinner. Afterward, when he was in there reading the newspaper, she'd asked him to hand her the box. This wasn't as good a method as having him actually handle the cards to imprint them with the forces of his life, but she hadn't wanted to be obvious. Now the cards were spread, and the ones she'd turned so far strongly indicated that danger surrounded him. "First you tell me that he's coming to help...that he's the only one who can help…and now you tell me his presence could mean trouble! I wish you'd make up your mind," she seethed under her breath.

"I suppose it's natural for a bride to talk to herself before the wedding."

Roxy jerked her gaze to the door of the sitting room to discover Eric standing there. Panic swept through her. He suddenly seemed much bigger than before and she recalled that just this afternoon Jamie had mentioned that Eric was teaching him karate.

Eric frowned at the fear he saw in her eyes. He'd been aware of Roxy's growing uneasiness. During dinner there had been a couple of times when he'd caught her glancing covertly at him, a worried shadow in her eyes. He'd told himself it was merely premarital jitters, but this was clearly a lot more serious than that. "Looks to me like we need to talk. It's obvious something is bothering you."

Her gaze flickered around seeking something within her reach that could be used as a weapon. "I just find it a little strange that you have no one to call and tell that you're getting married."

After years of surviving by being able to read other people, Eric recognized the signs. She was terrified of him and felt trapped. "My work wasn't the kind that encouraged the building of traditional friendships."

He took a step into the room and Roxy stiffened in preparation for a battle. "I thought you were in the military. It's always been my impression that men form strong buddy-buddy relationships there so that if they go into battle, they know who to trust to guard their backs."

Eric stopped his approach and stood frowning at her patronizingly. "I've been under your roof for nearly ten days. You proposed marriage to me and now you're suddenly afraid I'm some sort of pervert or psychopath?"

She continued to watch him, her body at the ready. "I never read the Tarot specifically for you before tonight."

Eric's gaze shifted to the cards. Apparently they'd revealed something that had scared her. "And what did they tell you?"

Her hand closed around a crystal paperweight. "They show danger lurking all around you."

His gaze returned to her and he studied her in a grim silence. He had two choices. He could walk away or he would have to tell her some truths about his life. If he walked away, she'd probably lose Jamie and two lives would be destroyed. If Maude was watching from above, she'd never forgive him for that. And he'd never forgive himself. When they'd applied for the license, he'd expected to be uneasy. Instead, every instinct had told him he was doing the right thing. Besides, The Unit had vanished. Still, he could not totally discount a need for secrecy. "I want your word that what I tell you will go no further."

"That's not a reassuring request. In the past when one of our boys was getting ready to tell a really big lie, he'd begin just that way."

His scowl darkened. "You do have a distrusting soul."

"It's from lessons learned the hard way."

Her attitude angered him. She seemed determined to believe the worst of him. His rational side could understand her behavior, but her distrust cut too deeply. "Well, I tried. I was willing to trust you, but apparently you're not willing to give me even the benefit of the doubt. To put your mind at ease, I'll be packed and out of here in the hour."

As he started to leave, Roxy experienced a rush of panic. She could lose everything. Besides, the cards hadn't actually indicated that he was a danger to her or

Jamie, simply that danger surrounded him. "Wait. You have my word. I'm willing to listen with an open mind."

Eric considered continuing his exit. He was not used to allowing either anger or lust to influence his judgment. Yet, where Roxy Dugan was concerned, he didn't seem to be able to control either of them fully. However, the fact that she was a difficult woman did not release him from the promise he'd made Jamie or his obligation to Maude. Turning back, he stood facing her. "My military records will say that I served in the military police at various locations about the globe and that the duty was uneventful until the incident in which I was injured. The truth is, I was in a special branch of the military police and the operations I was involved in were highly dangerous. As for my not having any close friends to call, the work I did was undercover. My life and the lives of my compatriots depended on our anonymity. We never knew each other's real names, nor did we socialize when we weren't on assignment."

In spite of the fact that this sounded like something out of a B spy movie, Roxy's instinct was to believe him, but the worry that she was letting her fear of losing Jamie influence her caused her to hesitate. She looked to the cards. Hoping they would give her a positive sign, she started to turn the next one over.

Eric reached her in one long stride. Capturing her wrist, he stopped her. "Don't look at the card. Look at me," he ordered. Why it was so important that she trust him on his word he didn't understand, but it was.

Roxy was startled by her lack of fear. Instead of his hold on her wrist feeding her terror, it was causing a sense of security and protectiveness to spread through her. Looking into the blue depths of his eyes, she heard herself saying, "If a man had anything criminal to hide, he'd be a fool to knowingly involve himself in a matter where he'd be investigated by the authorities to see if he's a fit father, and you're no fool.''

Eric nodded his satisfaction. "I'm glad we settled that.'' Releasing her, he strode from the room.

Continuing to sit motionless for a long moment after he disappeared from view, Roxy was aware of the lingering warmth left by his touch. Her attraction to him was growing stronger. Suddenly, again worried that she was letting emotion rather than reason rule her judgment, she looked at the card in her hand. It signified trustworthiness. Laying it down beside the others, she turned the rest of the cards. They showed a man of character and strength.

Still, she continued to be uneasy. Her intuitiveness insisted that the danger lurking around Eric was not in the past but in the present.

Was she placing herself and Jamie in jeopardy? Quickly she shuffled the cards and redealt them for herself. The lurking danger appeared there, as well. But the cards also implied that together, she, Jamie and Eric formed a strong triad capable of fighting off the danger.

She rose and paced the room, her motherly concern for Jamie nagging at her. The cards couldn't tell her the future. They told her only of the attributes and shortcomings of people and of possible danger or joy awaiting them in their lives and of alliances that would make them stronger or lead to destruction. But, in the final analysis, they could not predict the outcome of any action taken. She also knew that the triad the three of them formed wasn't invincible. Nothing was invincible.

But if she sent Eric away to protect Jamie, she would probably be throwing away her chance of gaining custody of the boy, in which case he could be in as much danger as any Eric might bring their way.

And there was the triad to consider. If she sent Eric away, on his own he might not be able to ward off any threat lurking around him. A protectiveness toward the man pervaded her. "He did come to Jamie's and my aid," she reasoned. And the cards did indicate that the three of them belonged together. Besides, she really didn't have a choice if she wanted to keep Jamie.

Still, her anxiousness about the decision to let Eric stay continued to torment her as she put the cards away and left the room. She was starting up the stairs when she changed direction. Seeking Eric out, she found him on the front porch. "I can't shake the feeling that the danger implied by the cards is current, not in the past," she said. "Could your past be catching up with you?"

Eric considered the possibility. He trusted Tobias's discretion, which made that possibility unlikely. Another reason for Roxy's feelings occurred to him. "Could it be future danger you're sensing?" he asked. "I've been considering what I'll do when I leave here and have concluded that regular military service isn't for me. I've had a job offer with a private investigative firm. If I don't take it, I'll try the FBI. Either choice will place me in the line of danger at one time or another."

Roxy breathed a sigh of relief. "That would explain the aura of danger surrounding you. You lived with it before you came here and when you leave you'll return to the same kind of life. It's a part of who you are."

Going up to bed a few minutes later, she realized that she'd misinterpreted the triad, as well. Eric would be out of Jamie's and her life by the time he returned to his former life-style. He wasn't the one the triad was protecting. It was Jamie.

Entering her room, she scolded herself for letting her emotions rule her logic. It was ridiculous to think that she and Jamie could offer Eric any protection beyond that which he could provide for himself.

A quirky half smile began to tilt one corner of her mouth. Her panic hadn't been entirely useless. She'd learned a lot about her future husband. "And a woman should know something about the man she's going to marry, even if the marriage is only temporary," she murmured.

Downstairs, Eric stood frowning at the night sky. Clearly, Roxy was no longer worried by the danger her cards had seen around him. As for himself, he still wasn't entirely convinced that the reading of Tarot cards had any validity. There were other reasons she could have seen him as in danger or dangerous. Her own fear of intimacy with a man could have made her think of him as dangerous. Or, knowing he was a military man and had been injured once, subconsciously she could have labeled his life as being one of danger.

However, as much as he wanted to, he couldn't completely overlook the cards. If there was some validity in her ability to read them and her original interpretation that there was danger lurking near at hand was right, he wasn't willing to risk Jamie's or her safety. Going in search of the card Tobias had given him, he found it and placed a call.

"It's good to hear your voice," Tobias said when he came to the phone. "Are you ready to come stay with me a while and let me talk you into coming to work for me?"

"I have some unfinished business here," Eric replied. "I'm getting married."

"That was a rather fast courtship," Tobias noted, surprise evident in his voice. "Or did you know your fiancée before you were shot?"

"I only met her a few days ago. It's not a love match.

I'm doing her a favor. She needs a husband so that she can adopt a child, a ten-year-old by the name of Jamie. He was one of the boys living at the home when it had to be closed.''

"In that case, you'll need references.'' Tobias's voice took on the tone of one who now understood why he'd received this call. "Well, don't worry. I'll write an outstanding recommendation for you and I can get others. We'll convince the authorities that you'll make a wonderful father.''

"Actually, I hadn't thought that far ahead. But you're right, I'll probably need those letters. However, they aren't the reason for this call.'' Eric paused for a second, then asked, "Can I talk freely over this line?''

"Yes.''

In his mind's eye Eric could see the elderly man, sitting more upright, prepared for action. Unwilling to tell him that it was a Tarot card reading that had prompted this call, Eric took another approach. "I've always had the utmost confidence in you, but I have to ask.... As you've already realized, the authorities will be investigating me. Is there any chance they could stumble onto the truth and expose my wife and the boy to danger from someone in my past?''

For a long moment Tobias was silent, then he said, "Normally I would issue an emphatic no. But during the Susan Irving matter, you were in the cold, out of the control of The Unit. Since she'd convinced you that she was to be your only contact and was manipulating your activities during that time, we had no way of finding out for certain what you did or who you met with. And since you have no memory of that period either, it remains in the dark. However, as I told you before, following Susan's death, no further inquiries were made concerning you, and that convinced us that your trail had been erased."

"I'm sure you're right." Mentally Eric kicked himself for even making the call. "I'm sorry I bothered you."

For a moment there was a silence, then Tobias said sternly, "There's something you aren't telling me."

"It's just premarital jitters," Eric hedged, still unwilling to mention the Tarot cards.

"You said the marriage was more of a business arrangement than the real thing. I think you should tell me what's really going on and why you're suddenly concerned about your past catching up with you," Tobias persisted.

Eric grimaced self-consciously. He knew by Tobias's tone that the man was not going to let this matter rest until he learned the truth. "I'm a little embarrassed to tell you the real reason I called."

"You're not a man who jumps at shadows. I want to know what prompted you to contact me."

"How do you feel about Tarot card readings?" Eric felt a flush building from his neck upward. He expected to hear a chuckle from the other end of the line. There was none.

Tobias's manner remained serious. "I've known some very important people who believed in such things. I, myself, once knew a reader with an uncanny talent for being correct. Do your instincts tell you that you can trust your reader?"

"My instinct is to trust the woman, but I find it hard to believe in a deck of cards. I just figured it wouldn't hurt to check with you."

"As I told you, as far as I know, all leaks were plugged." Concern entered Tobias's voice. "But like I said, I'm not infallible. Did your reader specifically say you were in danger?''

"She said the cards imply that danger surrounds me. However, she seems satisfied to believe I exude this aura because of the life-style I've chosen.''

Tobias's voice relaxed. ''That's very possible.''

"And about that life-style,'' Eric said, deciding that now was as good a time as any to discuss the future, ''I'm seriously considering the job offer you made me.''

"Wonderful! Do you want me to start the ball rolling to have your discharge from the military completed?''

"Yes.''

"I'll get on it first thing tomorrow morning,'' Tobias promised. A polite plea entered into his voice. ''Any chance I could get an invitation to the wedding? I'd like to meet your bride.''

Eric was surprised and pleased that Tobias would want to attend. ''The wedding's tomorrow at one o'clock in Zephyr, Pennsylvania, at the courthouse in Judge Blaire's chambers. If you can make it, that would be terrific.''

"I'll be there. And, if you don't mind, Hagen will accompany me. At my age, I rarely travel alone.''

Eric guessed that Hagen's company was more for security reasons than to nursemaid Tobias. Clearly Tobias's agency dealt with matters sensitive enough that ''The Old Man,'' as his former agents used to call him, had need to be somewhat cautious. Eric smiled to himself. That was just the kind of work he was looking for. Aloud he said, ''Hagen is welcome.'' He gave Tobias directions and was about to ring off when Tobias asked, ''By the way, what's the bride's name?''

"Roxanne Dugan. Maude left the farm to her.''

"Is she your Tarot reader, as well?''

Eric hesitated. He wasn't certain Roxy would want her

interest in the cards spread around, but then he'd never lied to Tobias and he wouldn't start now. "Yes."

"I'm now doubly interested in meeting her."

"It would be best if you don't mention the cards," Eric cautioned. "They are a private matter to her."

"I'll be very discreet," Tobias promised.

Hanging up a few minutes later, Eric smiled. Not only was he honored that Tobias wanted to come to the wedding, he'd have two guests so he wouldn't seem like such a loner to Roxy's family. He was also satisfied with Roxy's conclusion that the danger surrounding him was due merely to his choice of careers.

Returning the receiver to its cradle, Tobias rang for Hagen, then sat contemplating the fire blazing in the hearth. He remembered Roxanne Dugan well. Keeping Eric anonymous while acting on his behalf, Tobias and Hagen had paid her a visit after receiving the letter about Maude's death. Learning that the home would not be re-opened, they'd offered their condolences and left.

"Is something wrong?" Hagen asked, entering the room moments later.

"I'm not sure," Tobias replied. "You once asked me why I found Roxanne Dugan so interesting. At the time I didn't answer because I don't like to make brash judgments or claims." A sparkle entered his eyes. "When I met her, I sensed a specialness about her. There was even a hint of familiarity. Those two things caused me to wonder if her ancestry could be linked to ours. Now I'm beginning to believe I was right."

Hagen frowned thoughtfully at his granduncle. "And what has almost convinced you that she has Druid blood in her veins?"

"She reads the Tarot cards with enough confidence that

even a skeptic like Eric Bishop couldn't make himself totally discount what she says." He breathed an impatient sigh. "However, that isn't proof that she really has the talent. It just means that she believes she does."

"And how will you determine which is the truth?" Hagen asked.

"Only time will tell." The frown returned to Tobias's face. "In the meanwhile, I want you to pull the files on the Susan Irving case. I want to see if there is anyone we overlooked who could pose a threat to Eric."

"I thought that business was dead and buried."

"Most likely it is. But I want to take another look into the matter anyway." As Hagen started to the door, Tobias added, "And arrange for a private jet. We have a wedding to attend tomorrow in Zephyr, Pennsylvania."

Chapter Seven

"**I** now pronounce you man and wife. You may kiss the bride," Judge Blaire proclaimed, closing his book with a sharp slap to signify a job well done.

Her gaze on Eric dressed in his Sunday suit and looking more handsome than she'd ever imagined a man could look, Roxy tried to force a smile, but her muscles were too tense.

Having seen that same tautness in faces of companions just before they embarked on a mission of which they were uncertain, Eric smiled encouragingly and gave her a comradely wink. Clothed in a soft green pastel suit with lace on the lapels, she looked deliciously feminine, he thought as he bent to kiss her.

His wink and smile helped ease Roxy's tenseness and she found herself grinning back at him. At that moment his lips met hers. Their warmth heated her blood. Their touch weakened her knees. The contact lasted only seconds, but during that time every fiber of her being awakened and tingled with pleasure.

Lifting his head, Eric read the desire in her eyes. Erotic thoughts filled his mind. "Later," he whispered in her ear, husky promise in his voice.

Roxy's breath caught in her lungs. Excitement, nervousness and anticipation all swirled within her.

Behind a polite mask Eric hid a sudden bout of impatience to get her alone as he straightened away from her. He thanked the judge, then turned to face their guests. The gathering was small. Roxy's parents, Deborah and Charlie Dugan, were there, along with her maternal grandmother, Faye Swain, Jamie, Tobias and Hagen.

Roxy's heart was pounding wildly with excitement as she, too, thanked the judge. *Calm down, you're acting like you've never been with a man before,* she chided herself. Still, her blood continued to race as she turned to face their guests also.

She'd been surprised when Tobias Smith and Hagen Scanlon had arrived. Eric had mentioned that he'd invited two guests, but she hadn't expected those guests to be people she would recognize. Tobias and Hagen had entered at the last minute, just as the judge was preparing to begin, and there had been no time to exchange greetings. Now the elderly gentleman was approaching her, his hand extended.

"This is Tobias Smith, an old acquaintance and my soon-to-be employer. He runs the private investigative firm I mentioned," Eric said. "And Hagen Scanlon, another of his employees," he added as Hagen joined his granduncle.

Tobias took Roxy's hand in his in a warm greeting. "It's a pleasure to see you again."

She saw the surprise on Eric's face. "Mr. Smith came by the farm soon after Maude's death. He told me he was acting as a representative of one of her benefactors but he did not say who.''

"Because Eric couldn't come," Tobias explained, "I wanted to see if there was anything I could do on his behalf to aid you.''

The realization that while Eric was in a coma Mr. Smith had been involved in watching over his affairs piqued Roxy's interest. That kind of close association led her to reason that Mr. Smith probably had some knowledge of Eric's prior covert activities. That would explain his offer of a job in his firm. However, recalling that she'd vowed to be silent about Eric's former existence, she said nothing of her suspicions. Instead, she merely smiled and said, "Your concern was appreciated.''

"And you must be Jamie," Tobias said, turning his attention to the boy and extending his hand.

Jamie merely nodded and accepted the handshake.

Following that came a flurry of introductions between Tobias, Hagen and the rest of Roxy's family.

A polite but meaningful cough from the judge reminded them of his presence. "I need two witnesses to sign the license," he said, holding up a pen.

Charlie Dugan and Tobias performed that task. When it was completed, the judge glanced at his watch, then with apology in his voice, informed them that he had other business to attend to.

Immediately, they all thanked him and hurried out.

Arriving back at the farm, Roxy ordered Eric and Jamie to greet their guests while she went into the kitchen to set out the sandwich fixings she'd gathered for a light supper. She was taking a plate of cold cuts out of the refrigerator when her mother entered with a platter of fried chicken, followed by her grandmother with a bowl of potato salad and her father carrying a large bakery box.

"You can't have a wedding without a cake," Deborah Dugan said in answer to the question she read on her daughter's face. "I called Jackson's Bakery as soon as I hung up from talking to you."

Roxy grinned sheepishly. "A cake from Jackson's Bakery makes any occasion special." She recited what had become a family motto through the years. "Thanks, Mom."

"We're trying to think positive thoughts about this marriage," Deborah replied.

"Just put the cake right there," Faye Swain ordered Charlie Dugan, indicating with a nod of her head that she wanted the box set on the table. "Then go spend some time with your new son-in-law. I'm not leaving here until I'm satisfied Roxy hasn't gone and jumped from the frying pan into the fire."

"None of us are," Charlie replied over his shoulder as he made a quick exit.

Roxy frowned. "The cards are in Eric's favor. I thought you two trusted them."

"The talent to read the cards bypassed me. But I'm aware that it isn't an exact science and even someone as talented as you can make a mistake," Deborah replied. "All I know is that you've married a virtual stranger in order to adopt Jamie. And while your motives are worthwhile and Eric seems like a nice man, I'm not convinced this was a wise move." With curt pointedness, she added, "People aren't always what they seem, and your cards haven't always helped you make the right decisions in the past."

"If you're referring to Tom, the cards indicated that he had shortcomings, but then, no one is perfect. I'd known him all my life. I thought he loved me enough that he would come through for me when the going got tough. I was wrong.''

Faye regarded her granddaughter sternly. "Is it possible that in this instance you may have again overlooked some very important warnings?''

Roxy had been fairly certain her grandmother would not take her word for what the cards said. The sharp edge in Faye's voice told her that her assumption was correct. "Apparently you did your own reading.''

"Danger surrounds your husband,'' Faye said curtly.

"Before he came here, he was in the military police. His job was dangerous. When he leaves here, he'll be going to work for Tobias Smith as a private investigator. He has chosen a path fraught with danger. It is only natural the cards would reflect that. But the danger is his, not mine or Jamie's.''

"I suppose that could be the case,'' Faye conceded, her tone indicating that she wasn't entirely convinced.

"My reading also showed a triad between myself, Eric and Jamie,'' Roxy added. "It indicated a strength and rightness about this union.''

Faye breathed a disgruntled sigh. "I saw it, too. It was the only reason I didn't stand up and protest your marriage when the judge asked if there were any who objected.''

Knowing that her grandmother was only speaking out of loving concern, Roxy gave her a hug. Releasing her, she faced her levelly. "Jamie needs me, and I need Eric to get legal custody of Jamie. This will all work out.''

Deborah approached and took Roxy's hand in hers. "If anything should go wrong, your father and I are prepared to help you in any way we can.''

"Thanks.'' Roxy gave her mother a tight hug also.

"All three of us will be here for you,'' Faye interjected.

"I appreciate your support,'' Roxy said gratefully.

"But don't worry, I'm sure this will all work out just fine." Then, wanting to put an end to this discussion, she added, "And now we'd better get the food put out or the men will be coming in wanting to know if something is wrong."

Entering the living room a few minutes later to announce that the supper buffet was ready, she was surprised to discover Jamie talking with Tobias. Although the boy had begun to be more vocal, he still had a tendency to be standoffish with strangers. Yet he seemed at ease with the elderly gentleman.

Eric, however, didn't look comfortable at all. Her father had him cornered and was, she was certain, grilling him about his past.

Beginning to shoo the men into the kitchen to fill their plates, she hooked her arm protectively through Eric's and gave her father a warning glance to let him know that she wanted the inquisition stopped.

Charlie tossed back a "not until I'm satisfied" look, then preceded her and Eric into the kitchen.

"I'm really sorry," she apologized in a whisper.

"Has your father ever worked for the police?" Eric asked with a mischievous grin. "I don't think I've ever met anyone with more tenacity when he's after an answer."

"He's a schoolteacher."

Eric's grin broadened. "That explains a lot. I was a bit of a discipline problem in school. Teachers have a nose for sniffing us out, even years late."

She frowned up at him. "I'd have pictured you as the solemn, studious type."

He raised and lowered his eyebrows in Groucho Marx fashion. "I have a playful side."

There was a promise in his eyes that caused her blood to race. "I'm looking forward to meeting it."

Eric leaned nearer her ear and nipped the lobe. "I'm looking forward to introducing you."

Her breath locked in her lungs. "Behave," she ordered, adding in husky tones, "for now."

"Yes, ma'am." Pleased with the effect he was having on her, he continued to smile inwardly to himself while outwardly adopting an expression of polite interest in the array of food.

Feeling herself being watched, Roxy looked toward the head of the line where her mother and grandmother were pouring drinks and carrying them to the table for the men already seated with their plates of food. There was concern on the women's faces, and she knew they'd noticed the playful exchange between her and Eric.

During the meal, the cutting of the cake and the cleaning up afterward, she managed to keep too busy for them to get her alone. She didn't want to have to answer the questions she knew they wanted to ask. But trying to avoid them was like trying to stop the tide, she mused as her family prepared to leave and her mother and grandmother finally managed to corner her away from the men.

"I thought this was to be a marriage in name only," her mother said in lowered tones.

"It's a marriage, Mom," she replied.

"Does he know about the scarring?" Faye demanded anxiously.

"Yes."

"Knowing and seeing are two different things," Deborah cautioned. "I don't want you to go through what you did with Tom."

"I will never allow any man to hurt me the way he did," Roxy assured her.

Faye gave her granddaughter a hug, then made a bee-line for Eric. Drawing him aside, she said, "I know Roxy and Jamie belong together. And I know marrying you was the only way to assure that. But I'm still not certain I approve of this arrangement. You'd better treat my grand-daughter right or you'll be answering to me."

Roxy's mother and father had approached Eric also. Both had heard the threat and both had expressions on their faces that made the same promise as the one spoken by Faye Swain.

"You have my word I'll treat her well," Eric vowed.

Roxy had joined the group and was scowling at her family. "I'm really sorry about this." She again apolo-gized for their behavior.

"No need to be," Eric replied. His gaze rested on Faye momentarily, then traveled to Deborah and Charlie. "I envy my wife for having a family who cares so deeply for her."

"She has that," Charlie returned, his tone warning Eric never to forget it.

Roxy knew her family was trying to protect her, but hated the way they kept threatening her new husband. "You're going to get caught in rush-hour traffic if you don't leave now," she cautioned, taking her father's arm and guiding him toward the front door.

Reluctantly Faye and Deborah followed.

Pausing at the door, Charlie looked back at Tobias and Hagen, who had been standing a polite distance from the others, allowing Roxy's family privacy in which to say their farewells. "Are you sure I can't give you a lift some-where?" he offered.

Roxy, too, looked to her two remaining guests. Since the ceremony she'd been too busy to wonder about trans-portation for them. They'd ridden back to the farm with her family. Assuming they were expecting Eric to drive them to wherever they'd arranged for transport home, she experienced a jab of irritation. She didn't want to be parted from her new husband for even a short while. Stunned by this realization, she silently scowled at herself. Getting attached to him was not part of the plan!

"Thank you," Tobias replied. "But our ride should be arriving at any moment."

An increasing humming filled the air. As everyone exited onto the porch a helicopter came into view. It landed in the meadow, far enough away from the house so that no one was adversely affected by the draft from its propellers. Once on the ground, the pilot cut the motor.

Tobias waited until Roxy's family had finished their goodbyes and were driving away, then he and Hagen began their departure. They thanked Roxy and Eric for the invitation to the wedding, then both shook hands with Jamie. Again Roxy was surprised by how naturally the boy behaved with the two strangers. He actually seemed comfortable in their company. But then, so was she, she realized.

"I was wondering if you could give us a ride to the helicopter?" Tobias requested of Eric after congratulating him a final time.

"Sure thing," Eric replied.

"Can I ride along?" Jamie asked. "I've never seen a helicopter up close."

"If it's all right with Roxy, I can have the pilot take you up for a short ride," Tobias offered.

Jamie looked up at her pleadingly. "Please."

She'd never seen him so animated or behaving so naturally. "Sure."

Standing on the porch watching the men drive across the field in the truck, she had the feeling that Tobias had more on his mind than satisfying a child's wish. She'd seen a glance pass between the man and her husband that suggested Tobias wanted to talk to Eric alone. Going inside, she watched from the living-room window as the chopper took off with Jamie and Hagen inside. Immediately her gaze went back to the cab of the truck. She'd been right. Tobias and Eric looked to be having a serious conversation. She wondered if Tobias was giving Eric fatherly advice.

Her nose crinkled in a self-mocking grimace. "Most likely they're talking about when Eric can begin work," she muttered. This thought caused a sharp pang of regret.

"He could prove to be incredibly boring in bed and after tonight I'll be glad when he's gone," she told herself, attempting to nullify the sudden displeasure the thought of his leaving produced. In the next instant she was remembering the nip on her earlobe. A surge of heat curled through her. With it came an almost overwhelming jolt of nervousness.

"Just don't think about him. Concentrate on getting the house straightened," she ordered herself and, turning away from the window, began to busy herself with picking up any glasses left lying around.

In the truck, Tobias had waited until the helicopter was far enough away that he didn't have to shout, then said, "Just as a precaution, I'm reviewing the Susan Irving matter. However, as I've said before, since no one showed any interest in discovering your whereabouts nor were any further attempts made on your life after she was taken into custody, I assume your memories are of no importance to any of her associates."

"That does seem the most logical assumption," Eric agreed.

"However, blank spots always make me nervous. Have

you remembered anything yet? People you met? Places you stayed?"

Eric frowned. "That period of time is still foggy."

Tobias nodded. "If your wife is correct about the danger lurking around you, I'm inclined to believe her interpretation that it's your chosen life-style that has created the aura."

Mentally, Eric breathed a sigh of relief. "I agree. But thanks for looking into the matter anyway." A self-mocking grimace spread across his face. "I hope you don't think I'm a little nuts for letting some cards get to me?"

Tobias smiled reassuringly. "I assure you, I don't."

In that instant Eric knew that Tobias was a believer. Interesting, he mused. He'd always thought of his boss as being a man who believed only in fact.

"I have some friends in positions of authority who might be able to help speed the adoption process," Tobias said, changing the subject. "I'll speak to them."

Eric thanked him, then all conversation ceased as the helicopter descended.

Back at the farmhouse Roxy returned to the window and watched Jamie climb out of the helicopter and Tobias climb in. Then the machine was airborne and Eric and Jamie were on their way back to her. A sense of oneness filled her. It was as if the three of them together formed a single unit.

"Don't start thinking like that!" she admonished herself.

And she did manage to keep thoughts of them as a "forever" family out of her mind for the rest of the evening. But keeping under control thoughts of her and Eric and what lay ahead later that night was much more of a challenge. Anxiety mingled with a sense of adventure and anticipation.

And now the time for the "later" that Eric had promised was drawing near. Peeking in on Jamie to assure herself that he was asleep, she heard the sound of Eric's shower running. For one brief second she considered slipping in with him, but the romantic imp within her had been badly damaged by Tom and was not yet healed. Her more prudent side winning easily, she headed to the bathroom at the far end of the hall for a private shower. As she soaped herself, the sight of her scarring caused a fresh bout of nerves.

"He's seen it," she reminded herself, using the sound of her voice to give herself courage. And it worked.

But not for long. A few minutes later, as she pulled on her simple white cotton nightgown, uncertainty again plagued her. Maybe she should have gotten out one of the lacy, sexy gowns stored in the bottom drawer of her dresser. This thought caused one of her back muscles to knot. She hadn't worn any of those since the night Tom had blurted out that he couldn't bear the sight of her.

"This gown will do just fine," she told herself.

Pushing the memory of Tom from her mind, she brushed her hair, then dabbed on a bare touch of perfume. "And now for the moment of reckoning," she murmured under her breath, leaving the bathroom.

Entering her bedroom, she came to an abrupt halt. Eric wasn't there. Had he changed his mind about consummating their marriage? She realized that although she'd tried to deny this fear, it was what had been the real basis for her nervousness all evening. Without even realizing it, she'd been bracing herself to face his rejection. Her shoulders straightened. She'd been doing just fine without male companionship, and if he had changed his mind she'd continue to do just fine. Still, hot tears burned at the back of her eyes. "I will never, never, never set myself up for this kind of humiliation again," she vowed through clenched teeth.

Footsteps sounded in the hall and her facial muscles hurt as she forced them into a facade of indifference. *He'll probably say something like…I've decided it'd be best if we keep this strictly business,* she mused dryly. As the door swung open, her body stiffened until it felt brittle. Then she saw the laden tray he was carrying and her eyes rounded in surprise. There was a bottle of champagne in a silver ice bucket and a plate with crackers, cheese and caviar.

"The caviar, champagne and ice bucket are a special surprise from Tobias," he said, setting the tray on the small table in front of the window. "Jamie brought them back from the helicopter and we kept them a secret so that I could surprise you. I wasn't certain if you liked caviar, so I added the cheese." Eric hadn't been this nervous since he was a teenager. He'd been with women before, but this was different. Roxy had been through a lot and it was important to him that he perform well for her. *Or maybe it isn't her at all,* he mocked himself. Maybe it was his ego. Maybe he was worried that after three years in a coma, he wasn't as virile as he'd been before.

"How romantic," she said around the lump in her throat. She'd been so certain that this kind of evening would never be hers again. He was wearing only a pair of sweatpants, and her gaze traveled to his broad shoulders and chest. His muscles had once again gained definition and the fires of desire sparked to life within her.

Smiling at the heat he saw in her eyes, Eric popped the

PLAY "LUCKY 7" AND GET
FIVE FREE GIFTS!

HOW TO PLAY:

1. With a coin, carefully scratch off the silver box at the right. Then check the claim chart to see what we have for you—**FREE BOOKS** and a gift—**ALL YOURS! ALL FREE!**

2. Send back this card and you'll receive brand-new Silhouette Romance™ novels. These books have a cover price of $3.25 each, but they are yours to keep absolutely free.

3. There's no catch. You're under no obligation to buy anything. We charge nothing— ZERO—for your first shipment And you don't have to make any minimum number of purchases—not even one!

4. The fact is thousands of readers enjoy receiving books by mail from the Silhouette Reader Service™ months before they're available in stores. They like the convenience of home delivery and they love our discount prices!

5. We hope that after receiving your free books you'll want to remain a subscriber. But the choice is yours—to continue or cancel, any time at all! So why not take us up on our invitation, with no risk of any kind. You'll be glad you did!

YOURS FREE!

This lovely necklace will add glamour to your most elegant outfit! Its cobra-link chain is a generous 18" long, and its lustrous simulated cultured pearl is mounted in an attractive pendant! Best of all, it's ABSOLUTELY FREE, just for accepting our NO-RISK offer.

NOT ACTUAL SIZE

The Silhouette Reader Service™ — Here's how it works

Accepting free books places you under no obligation to buy anything. You may keep the books and gift and return the shipping statement marked "cancel." If you do not cancel, about a month later we'll send you 6 additional novels, and bill you just $2.67 each, plus 25¢ delivery per book and applicable sales tax, if any.* That's the complete price—and compared to cover prices of $3.25 each—quite a bargain! You may cancel at any time, but if you choose to continue, every month we'll send you 6 more books, which you may either purchase at the discount price...or return to us and cancel your subscription.

*Terms and prices subject to change without notice. Sales tax applicable in N.Y.

If offer card is missing write to: Silhouette Reader Service, 3010 Walden Ave., P.O. Box 1867, Buffalo, NY 14240-1867

BUSINESS REPLY MAIL

FIRST-CLASS MAIL   PERMIT NO. 717   BUFFALO, NY

POSTAGE WILL BE PAID BY ADDRESSEE

SILHOUETTE READER SERVICE
3010 WALDEN AVE
PO BOX 1867
BUFFALO NY 14240-9952

NO POSTAGE
NECESSARY
IF MAILED
IN THE
UNITED STATES

cork on the champagne and poured them each a glass. "To the success of our endeavor," he toasted.

"To success," she parroted. The sparkling wine tasted delicious. That and nerves caused her to drink it down in one gulp.

Eric poured her another glass. "Sip," he ordered. "I want you relaxed, not limp."

"I am a little tense," she confessed, obeying his instructions.

He piled some caviar on a small cracker and held it near her mouth. "Try a taste."

She opened her mouth and he slid the cracker inside. "Salty but nice," she said, after washing it down with a sip of champagne.

He fixed a cracker for himself and ate it. "Not bad."

Seeing a shadow of uncertainty flicker across his face, she squared her shoulders with pride. He wasn't toying romantically, he was procrastinating! "If you've changed your mind about our being intimate, I wish you'd just say so. I don't want you feeling you have to force yourself to go to bed with me."

A sheepish expression spread over his features. "It's not that. I'm just a little nervous. It's been a long time and I want to do this right." He set his glass on the table, then took hers from her and set it beside his.

Roxy stood nervously waiting for his next move.

Taking her hand, he carried it up to his lips and kissed her fingertips, then began working his way up her arm.

Her heart pounded furiously, sending her blood racing. "Nice beginning," she said, marveling that she was able to speak at all.

Reaching the short sleeve of her gown, he skipped to her neck, then trailed kisses to her lips. She tasted even more delicious than before, he thought as he claimed her mouth.

Roxy felt desirable. It was a delicious, vibrant sensation that began deep within and worked its way into every fiber of her being.

"Just follow my lead," Eric ordered gruffly. "Left leg first." Holding her tightly against him, he hummed a tango in her ear.

She'd never danced to that kind of music before, but skill wasn't necessary, she realized as she simply kept her legs pressed against his and moved in unison with his movements. With their bodies so molded together she could feel the strength of his thighs and was aware of his growing maleness. Exotic pleasure washed through her. A nervous giggle escaped when his hand moved below the small of her back and pressed her even more securely against him. "This is definitely a dance to be done in private," she murmured in his ear.

They had reached the bed. "We've had our appetizer and our turn on the floor," he said, kissing her lightly on the face. "Now it's time for the entrée." Releasing her, he tossed back the covers. "And you get to be the entrée," he added, kneeling in front of her.

She again stiffened as he trailed kisses up her leg, working the nightgown upward as he went. When he reached the scarring, he kissed it, too. Sensing no hesitation in his movement, she again relaxed, letting herself enjoy the feel of his touch as he continued his exploration until he had slipped the nightgown completely from her.

"You do make being the main course a very pleasant experience," she said, then gasped for breath as he cupped a breast and kissed the hardened nipple.

"And you make a delicious main course," he returned,

lifting her into his arms and laying her on the bed. Then, discarding his sweatpants, he joined her.

As their bodies entwined, Roxy became lost in a world of sensations. She felt more alive than she had in a long time and realized how much she'd missed this kind of intimacy.

Eric was amazed by the way their movements flowed together. She made making love to her so very easy.

"Now," Roxy whispered in his ear, her voice begging him to claim her fully.

Feeling like a man taking possession of what was rightfully his, he answered her plea. Lost in the womanly feel of her, he carried her with him to the zenith of their union.

"You are very good at this," Roxy said when they'd both been sated and her breathing finally became more normal again.

They were lying side by side on their backs. Turning onto his side, he levered himself on an elbow. "You made it easy." Recalling how she'd stiffened briefly when he'd reached her scarring during the disrobing, he added, "Your ex-husband was a jerk."

She smiled crookedly. "Thanks. I needed to hear that from someone else besides me and my family."

He kissed the tip of her nose. To his amazement, desire was again building. "How about dessert?"

"I thought you'd never ask," she returned, marveling that she could be so ready again so quickly.

Chapter Eight

Eric woke alert, his body tensed for action. He recognized the cause immediately. Many times in the past, a primitive instinct deep within had warned him when death threatened. It was that instinct that had woken him.

He lay still, listening. He heard nothing but Roxy's gentle breathing, then he realized that it was what he didn't hear that was important. He didn't hear the insects. Something or someone had quelled their chirping. A soft thud caught his attention.

He placed a hand over Roxy's mouth, then woke her.

She looked up at him in groggy confusion.

"We have an intruder," he said in her ear.

His words brought her acutely awake. "Are you sure it isn't Jamie wandering around the house?" she whispered back when he released his hold over her mouth.

"Whoever it is came from outside. Call the police." Slipping out of bed, he grabbed up his sweatpants and pulled them on.

Roxy picked up the receiver, to hear nothing but silence. "The line's dead," she whispered, panic spreading through her.

The frown on Eric's face deepened. Their night caller was a professional. A creaking sound reached his ears. It was the third step from the bottom of the staircase. Thank goodness old habits die hard, he thought. Rule number one when entering a new environment: Learn all you can about it. By the second day he'd been in this house, he'd taught himself to recognize all the sounds it made.

In the moonlight coming through the window, Roxy saw him raise a finger to his lips, cautioning her to be silent. With a wave of his hand, he motioned for her to get out of the bed and go into the closet. Obeying, she rose, lifted her nightgown from the floor and pulled it on before heading to the closet.

Eric placed pillows where they each had lain and covered them with the sheet, then he made his way to the door and flattened himself against the wall.

Roxy had started to the closet when she suddenly froze as fear for Jamie spread through her. She listened. To her relief, she didn't hear the squeaky floorboard in the hall near his room. She did hear a slight rustle and knew the intruder was coming their way.

Seeing her still in the bedroom and realizing their night caller had reached their door, Eric frantically motioned for her to lie on the floor.

She obeyed. As the door was slowly pushed fully open, she saw a large dark form and a glint of silver. Their uninvited caller had a gun. The barrel seemed extra long, she thought, then realized the weapon had a silencer. At least, it looked like the ones she'd seen in the movies.

There were several slight whizzing sounds, each followed by a pop as if someone had punched a pillow. Next came a startled gasp followed by something hitting the floor, then the black-clothed body came flying across the room. Jumping up, she switched on the light, to see Eric and the ski-masked intruder squaring off like two fighters in a karate movie. The gun lay on the floor just inside the door and there were round holes in Eric's and her pillows.

In the next instant Eric and the intruder were locked in combat. A chair was knocked over, followed by the table by the window.

Hearing footsteps running up the stairs, again fear for Jamie raced through her. Making her way around the men, she ran into the hall just in time to encounter a second black-clothed intruder.

"Just stay where you are, lady," he ordered, a gun leveled at her chest.

"Roxy!" Jamie called out in panic, racing toward them.

The man swung around.

Without even thinking, Roxy ran into him as hard as she could, shoving him down. The gun went flying out of his hand. Grabbing up a vase from the hall table, she hit him over the head when he tried to rise. With a groan, he sank back down to the floor.

"Are you two all right?" Eric asked, coming out of the bedroom.

"What happened?" Jamie demanded, his voice laced with fear.

"We had a couple of robbers, but we handled them," Eric replied in soothing tones. He ruffled the boy's hair. "Seems we make a good team."

Roxy reached for the hall light switch.

Eric caught her wrist. "Just in case these fellows have buddies, I think it would be best if we kept them in the dark as much as possible. You two get dressed while I tie these two up. Then we'll drive into town and get the police.'' He again ruffled Jamie's hair. "You can dress in the dark, can't you?"

"Sure," the boy replied.

"Go," Eric ordered. Turning to Roxy, he said, "I could use a flashlight and some nylons."

"There's a flashlight in the bottom of the bedstand on my side of the bed," she replied over her shoulder as she hurried into their room.

While she grabbed the hose out of her drawer, he found the flashlight and turned off the lamp. "Now get dressed," he ordered.

By the time she'd pulled on a pair of jeans, a sweatshirt and sneakers, he'd finished with the man in the hall and was tying up the one he'd left unconscious in the bedroom. She saw him pull off the man's ski mask and take a good look at his face and guessed he'd done the same with the one in the hall.

"I'm ready," Jamie said, suddenly appearing in their doorway.

Eric took a minute to pull on a shirt and some sneakers, then, picking up the men's guns, he held them at the ready while leading Roxy and Jamie down the stairs.

The truck was parked out front. Motioning for Jamie and Roxy to stand pressed against the hall wall, he peered out the nearest window. He saw no one. Closing his eyes, he listened. To his relief, he heard insects. "I don't think there's anyone out there," he said. "But just in case, I'm going to get the truck started, then I want the two of you to run as fast as you can and climb in."

The thought of him being injured caused Roxy's stomach to knot. She touched his arm, not to get his attention but because she wanted the physical contact. "Be careful," she said.

"Careful is my middle name," he replied, pleased by the concern he heard in her voice.

"I doubt that very much," she murmured worriedly as he slipped out the door and headed to the truck.

Jamie's hold on her hand tightened. "He'll be fine. He knows what he's doing. We just need to do what he says."

The trust she heard in the boy's voice confirmed what she'd begun to realize. Jamie had developed a strong bond with Eric. How would the boy handle Eric's leaving? *We'll cross that bridge when we come to it,* she told herself. Right now she needed to concentrate on getting away from here safely.

The motor of the truck shattered the silence of the night.

"Come on," Jamie said, jerking her hand.

They raced out of the house and climbed into the truck. Immediately Eric stepped on the gas and they took off at top speed for town.

"This time I helped, didn't I?" Jamie said, looking to Roxy and then to Eric for confirmation.

The three of them were alone in the office of Clark McMurphy, Zephyr's chief of police. Through the large window in the wall of the chief's office that allowed him to observe the activities in the main section of the police station, Roxy had been watching him talk on the radio and guessed he was speaking to the patrolmen and ambulance attendants he'd sent out to the farm. Now her attention turned to Jamie. "Yes, you did."

"You did great," Eric assured him with a warm smile.

As the boy smiled back, Roxy suddenly realized that the hauntedness that had lingered in his eyes—even after she and Eric had tried to convince him that what happened between his parents hadn't been his fault—was gone. As terrifying as this night had been, it had provided a way for Jamie to vindicate himself to himself. "You did really, really great," she said, and kissed him on the cheek.

Eric glanced through the window. Seeing the chief still busy on the radio, he said, "I'm going to call Tobias." His gaze leveled on Roxy. "He'll arrange a safe place for you and Jamie until this business is sorted out."

Roxy nodded as he punched in a number. Those men hadn't been robbers. They'd come to murder her and Eric and most likely Jamie, as well. Her instinct that the danger lurking around Eric was immediate had been right. If anything happened to Jamie because she had ignored the warnings, she would never forgive herself.

Although Roxy had expressed no anger toward him, Eric saw the slight tightening of her jaw and guessed she was mentally kicking herself for having invited him into her life. If he'd been in her shoes, he sure would be. But what was done was done. Hagen's voice on the other end of the line reminded him of his immediate business. "This is Eric Bishop," he said. "There was a murder attempt at the farm tonight. I need sanctuary for my wife and son." For an instant he was startled by how natural the words *wife* and *son* had sounded. "I didn't know who else to call. I figured Tobias could pass the word on to the appropriate party."

"Tobias will be pleased you called," Hagen replied. "Where are you?"

"The police station in Zephyr, Pennsylvania," he replied, then added, "Also, inform Tobias that I left two men tied up at the farm. The police chief has sent out an ambulance along with some officers to take them into custody."

"Stay where you are. Someone will be coming for you and your family," Hagen said, and rang off.

Eric was returning the receiver to its cradle when the chief entered, along with another officer. "Hope you don't mind. I needed to make a call," Eric said.

"No problem," the chief replied. "My officers found your intruders groggy and still securely tied. They're being transported to the hospital."

"Even unarmed they could be dangerous." Eric repeated the warning he'd given the chief when they'd first arrived. "I hope you've cautioned your men to be careful and to keep the prisoners handcuffed at all times."

"My men are professionals," the chief replied coolly. Then turning to Jamie, he smiled a fatherly smile. "You look as if you could use a soda. Why don't you go with Officer Nolan here." He paused to nod toward the female officer who had entered with him. "She'll get you one."

Jamie's hold on Roxy's hand tightened. "I'm not thirsty."

"Run along with the officer," Eric coaxed, guessing the chief had some questions he wanted to ask that he didn't want the boy hearing.

Following Eric's lead, Roxy said, "We just have to give the chief a statement. You run along."

A wave of protectiveness washed over Eric as Jamie rose reluctantly. His gaze locked on Officer Nolan and he nodded toward the view beyond the chief's window. "You'll keep him where my wife can see him at all times? She's been through a lot and I don't want her to worry."

The officer looked to her chief.

"Keep the boy where Roxy can see him," the chief ordered.

"Thanks," Roxy said, relieved that Jamie would not be out of her sight. But the relief was only partial. She was sure Eric had made the request because he, too, wanted to keep an eye on the boy, and the realization that the danger they were in was not over struck her full force again.

As soon as the door closed behind Officer Nolan and the boy, the chief rounded his desk, sat down and studied Eric narrowly. "There's more to this business than you're telling me. These weapons..." He paused to nod toward the two guns lying on his desk. "These weapons are pretty fancy for a couple of burglars. In fact, I've never known a burglar to use a silencer. And my men tell me there were a couple of pillows on the bed that had been shot full of holes."

"During my time in the military police, I could have made a few enemies," Eric replied noncommittally.

The chief looked to Roxy. "You and Maude did good work out at that farm, but some of the boys had trouble bred into them." His attention returned to Eric. "This has the look of a professional hit to me. Your military record is clean, but that doesn't mean you are. I'd hate to think you've involved Roxy in something dirty."

Eric's shoulders squared. "I'm a law-abiding citizen and I would never have come back here to Zephyr if I'd had any inkling I'd bring trouble along with me."

The phone rang. Continuing to regard Eric suspiciously, the chief lifted the receiver. "I told you to hold all my calls," he barked. Abruptly, his jaw tensed and whatever else he was going to say remained unsaid as he listened to what the person on the other end of the line was saying. Then with a gruff "I'll tell my men to expect you," he hung up.

Roxy watched nervously as the chief studied Eric in a stony silence. "Is something wrong?" she asked finally, unable to bear the building tension any longer.

The chief punched a button on his intercom. "Call the hospital. Tell our men that a couple of Federal agents will be coming to pick up the prisoners." Releasing the button, the chief again leveled his gaze on Eric. "I don't suppose that call you made had anything to do with this?"

Outwardly, Eric simply shrugged as if he knew nothing. Inwardly, he noted that Tobias apparently still had a lot of friends who would act quickly on his word.

"All right. So let's say I buy the fact that you're on the right side of the law. Tell me, are you expecting any more of these lethal types to be showing up in these parts?" the chief demanded. "Can't say as I'm worried about you. It's obvious you know how to take care of yourself. But I wouldn't want to see Roxy or the boy hurt. And I don't want any of my other citizenry caught in the cross fire, either."

"I've made arrangements for Roxy, Jamie and myself to move to a location away from here," Eric assured him.

The chief nodded his satisfaction.

Eric's gaze hardened with purpose. "I intend to report this as a simple burglary by a couple of sadistic sociopaths."

"And I suppose the Feds will back you up by saying they've been following this pair across several states? Or maybe they won't bother to tell me anything."

Uncertain how the matter would be handled, Eric merely shrugged.

For another long moment the chief studied Eric, then his scowl was replaced with a businesslike demeanor. "As long as you're out of my jurisdiction by dawn, I don't give a damn what you or they want to say about this. As far as I'm concerned, the case is closed."

"Thanks," Eric replied.

The chief looked to Roxy. "I thought you had more

sense than to get messed up in something like this...whatever *this* is."

Mentally Roxy agreed with him, but it was too late to turn back now. "I'm sure we'll be fine," she said, using positive thinking in an attempt to bolster her courage.

The chief shook his head and again, punched the button on his intercom. "Fran, I need you to come in here and take a statement from Mr. and Mrs. Bishop about the break-in at their place."

It was barely an hour later when Jamie, Roxy and Eric left Zephyr in the helicopter arranged for by Tobias. They were flown to a private airstrip several miles to the west, where they boarded a small plane.

"Tobias requested that you be brought to his estate for sanctuary," the pilot informed them as they boarded. "Someone will be dispatched to the farm to pack a few things for you. It was agreed by all parties that you should be transported to a safe haven as quickly as possible."

"Thanks," Eric replied.

The pilot nodded, then headed into the cockpit.

"I'm really sorry about all of this," he apologized to Roxy and Jamie as the plane became airborne.

Seated between them, Jamie took hold of a hand from each of them. "We're a team," he said proudly.

This experience had definitely had its rewards for the boy, Roxy admitted, trying to ease her guilt for having brought him into this. "I doubt very many women can claim to have had as much excitement on their wedding night," she quipped, determined for Jamie's sake to exhibit an upbeat attitude.

Eric would have understood if they'd been angry with him. He was furious with himself for getting them involved in this life-threatening situation. Of course, he hadn't done it on purpose. He'd thought he was safe. Still, they were in danger and it was because of him. The fact that neither appeared to hold it against him caused a curious stirring deep within. For the first time, he knew what it must be like for those who had families they could turn to in times of trouble.

Glancing down at Jamie, he saw the boy was already dozing, clearly exhausted by the events of the night.

In lowered tones he said to Roxy, "I really appreciate you taking this so well."

"It's not your fault I refused to heed the warnings given me," she replied. "I honestly thought marrying you was the best way to achieve Jamie's and my goal."

So much for that "family" feeling, Eric chided himself. She wasn't angry with him, because she was blaming herself for using bad judgment. As soon as she'd gained legal custody of Jamie and Tobias had helped him clean up this threat, he didn't doubt for a moment that she'd take Jamie and put as much distance between them and him as possible. But then, for him to disappear from their lives had been the original plan, he reminded himself. And it was what he wanted. He'd never been one to be tied down, and he didn't need to be worrying about anyone waiting back home when he was out on assignment. That could take away his edge. Leaning back, he dozed.

Recalling the triad, Roxy covertly studied the taut line of Eric's jaw. If she and Jamie hadn't been there to take out the second gunman, he would most likely be dead. That thought shook her to the core and she realized she felt the same amount of protectiveness toward him as she did toward Jamie. She also realized something else. At this moment she felt totally safe. That didn't seem rational but she did. *I'm probably in shock and I feel secure because we're putting distance between us and those men,* she reasoned. Then exhaustion overcoming her, she, too, slept.

Roxy watched the tall iron gates swing open to allow the car that had picked them up at the small private airport access to the tree-lined driveway beyond. Passing through the gates, she noticed a small caretaker's cottage. Then her attention was claimed by the huge, three-story, brick, colonial-style mansion ahead. She glanced toward Jamie and saw her own awe reflected on his face. She'd seen estates like this on television, but she'd never expected to be invited to stay at one.

Looking to Eric, she read no surprise on his face and realized that he'd moved in a stratum of society she'd never dreamed of ever being a part of.

"Mrs. Gibbons, my housekeeper, has arranged for a breakfast buffet," Tobias said, coming out to greet them as they climbed out of the car. "You must have a little something to eat, then I suspect you'll want to bathe and get some rest."

Accompanying Tobias into the dining room, Roxy didn't think she was hungry until the aroma of hot food drifted to her. Suddenly she was famished.

While they ate, Tobias made polite conversation, telling them that he was glad they'd escaped their ordeal unscathed and expressing the hope that they'd had a pleasant trip to his home. He seemed, Roxy thought, totally at ease, relaxed as if they were merely here on a friendly visit. But as they finished their meal, she noted a subtle change in Tobias. A flicker of impatience escaped from behind their host's polite mask.

"Mrs. Gibbons will show you and Jamie to your rooms," he said. "I need to speak to Eric for a moment before he joins you."

Again Roxy found herself hating being parted from her husband. *Get your emotions under control, girl,* she admonished herself, frustrated that even tonight's events hadn't curbed her growing feelings for him. She wanted to provide a stable environment for Jamie. Remaining with Eric Bishop was not going to accomplish that goal. Besides, remaining with Eric wasn't even an option. He wasn't in the market for a permanent family. Uninvited, the triad popped into her mind once again. *Don't even think about it,* she ordered herself, following Mrs. Gibbons up the stairs.

Assured that Roxy and Jamie were in safe hands, Eric accompanied Tobias into his study. "I assume you had something to do with the Feds who came to claim the prisoners," he said as soon as they were alone.

Tobias nodded. "I called in a favor. You were one of my recruits. As far as I'm concerned, if this has anything to do with your time in The Unit, it's my responsibility."

Eric experienced a sense of relief knowing that The Old Man would be helping. "I'm certain the one I tangled with in the bedroom was the shooter who nailed me at the airport three years ago."

Tobias nodded. "Clearly this has something to do with the Susan Irving case."

"But why wait until now? Why didn't whoever ordered this hit take me out sooner?"

"Maybe they only just found out you were alive. We did spread the word that you were dead."

"Maybe no one hired them," Eric hypothesized. "Maybe my hitter somehow discovered he'd botched the job and, being a professional, figured he still owed Susan a kill."

"In which case, he would have taken you out but he

wouldn't have tried to take out Roxy as well. He hadn't been paid for her."

"You're right," Eric agreed.

"Are you up to facing your intruders?"

Eric was unable to hide his surprise. "They're here?"

"Not far away." Tobias opened the French doors. "They asked to speak to me personally. The agents who picked them up designated Washington, D.C., as their destination, then brought them here. For a while, anyway, it will appear as if they disappeared into thin air."

Beyond the doors, Eric saw a jeep with Hagen at the wheel.

Leaving the manicured gardens behind, they traveled down an old logging road that was more ruts than road. Emerging into a clearing, Eric saw a helicopter pad and, not far from it, the entrance to a concrete bunker built into the mountain.

Entering, they were greeted by two men in suits. Eric knew they were government agents, but he didn't even try to guess what branch they worked for. "Which one do you want to see first?" one of the men asked, respect for Tobias evident in his voice.

Tobias turned to Eric. "You choose."

Looking through the small peephole in the first door, Eric saw the boyish, innocent-appearing shooter who had wounded him years earlier and tried to finish the job last night. He was sitting at the table in the middle of the room, his feet propped up, his manner calm as if he had no worries in the world. Sensing he was being watched, he looked toward the door. His eyes were as cold as a winter's night. "This one," he said.

"His name's Alvin Karr," one of the men in suits informed them before opening the door. "Looks like a kid, but he's thirty-two years old. No priors, but he matches the description of a pro Interpol has been looking for. They have someone on his way across the Atlantic now."

As Tobias and Eric entered the room, Alvin rose. "It's about time."

"Why did you want to speak to me?" Tobias asked. "I don't believe we've ever met before."

Alvin scowled with impatience. "Because you're the only one who can help me and you know it."

"I'm surprised you have so much confidence in me after my failure to protect Susan Irving. You do remember Miss Irving, don't you? You worked for her."

Alvin sneered. "She threw you a few crumbs to make you think she was cooperating. She was just buying time. She thought she could trust the clever Mr. CW to get her out. What she didn't realize was that as far as he was concerned, she'd become a liability. She'd been uncovered and she knew too much. Now me, I know the guy better than that. We're all expendable in his eyes. I want a deal. I tell you everything I know, and you help me disappear."

"All right. But I need a name, not initials."

"Don't have one. The CW stands for Computer Whiz. It was Susan's name for him. She told me I didn't need to know his real one or anything about him. She was the only one he made direct contact with. Even after she was dead, he still kept his association with me strictly a phone conversation with his voice electronically masked."

"Then why should he worry about you?" Tobias asked.

"He doesn't like loose ends. I know he exists. That's enough for him."

"I need something to go on. You could be making all of this up to get yourself a deal."

"If I'm making this up, then how'd I find out about

Bishop? Hell, even Susan didn't know his real name. We only knew his code name. And word was that my target had gone down. I had no reason to believe the John Doe file you fixed up to look like his wasn't for real.''

"Maybe you took a closer look, discovered something that didn't seem right and kept looking. You're a pro and you'd been hired to do a job. If he was still alive, the job was unfinished.''

"I thought the job was finished," Alvin growled. "But not Mr. CW. He doesn't trust anyone. He flipped through files, found some custodian who was in need of cash and found out from him that they'd moved one of the high-risk patients out of the hospital the night Bishop was supposed to have died. Then he began checking private clinics you guys might use. Since I could eyeball the target, he made me personally take a look at every patient admitted on the night the mystery patient was taken out of the hospital. Took me a few days, but I found him.''

"Why didn't you take Bishop out as soon as you found him?" Tobias asked.

"Mr. Whiz wanted the Susan Irving case closed. Once she was dead, he wanted it to look as if that was the end of it. He'd tapped into the computer system at the clinic and knew Bishop was in a coma." Alvin's gaze shifted to Eric. "He figured you'd eventually die on your own. When you came around, he notified me. He'd read your file and knew you had amnesia and couldn't remember the months before the shooting, so he told me to keep an eye on you and bide my time. I was supposed to eventually stage an accident so that your death would look natural. He ordered me to move cautiously. He said that even if you did start remembering, whatever it was he didn't want remembered was something you probably wouldn't recognize as important for a while. So Jazz and

I staked out the farm. Mr. CW had supplied us with some real sophisticated listening devices we could use from a distance. Everything was going great.''

Alvin suddenly smirked. "Then you went and called Tobias because of that loony you married and her Tarot cards.''

Eric had to struggle to keep from growling out that his wife was not a loony. Instead, he noted dryly, "Apparently your Mr. CW isn't as cynical as you where reading the cards is concerned.''

Alvin's smirk broadened. "It wasn't the cards. It was you and Tobias staying so cozy and you going to work for him. That made Mr. Whiz real antsy. He ordered the hit as quickly as possible. He knew Jamie Jordon's history. He told us to take you and the woman out on your wedding night and leave the gun behind. He figured the police would blame the boy. They'd assume he heard you and the missus fooling around, had a flashback to his youth and went in shooting, thinking he was saving her and ending up killing you both.''

"Nice guy,'' Eric muttered sarcastically.

"How do I find him?'' Tobias demanded.

Alvin shrugged. "I don't know. All I know is that if anyone can protect me from him it's you. I've lived up to my part of the bargain. Now you live up to yours. I want to be completely erased. I want a new name, a new face, the works.''

"Sorry. Can't do that.''

Alvin stiffened in shock. "You gave me your word.''

"I had my fingers crossed. Besides, you didn't give me any useful information.''

"I heard you were an honorable man.''

Tobias glared at him. "You tried to murder one of my people, not once but twice. If I were you, I'd confess any

European murders to the man from Interpol and hope the U.S. authorities are willing to turn you over to him.''

Panic spread over Alvin's features. "It doesn't matter where I go in the world. If they have computers, he can find me.''

"Then you better hope I find him first,'' Tobias replied. "Let me know if you think of anything that might help.''

"I've told you everything I know,'' Alvin growled. "And I told you in good faith. You owe me.''

Tobias made no response except to motion for Eric to knock on the door, signaling they wanted to leave.

Next they interviewed Alvin's partner, but Persy Connerson, known as Jazz, knew even less than Alvin. He was, however, equally frightened of the man he'd worked for.

"Looks like I did let the big one get away three years ago,'' Tobias muttered as they headed back to the manor house. "But the drug dealing and munitions thefts on our military bases did die down for a while. When they started back up, we all figured it was an entirely new set of entrepreneurs working independently of anything Susan had done.''

Eric paid little attention to Tobias's self-recriminations. He was trying to remember those last months before he'd lapsed into a coma. They continued to remain foggy.

"Get some rest,'' Tobias ordered when they reached the house. "I choose my people for their strength of mind. No one can hypnotize you. However, self-hypnotism isn't out of the question. After your mind has had a chance to rest, we'll try some relaxation techniques that might help you remember whatever it is you know.''

Eric didn't argue. Not only was he tired, he wanted to assure himself that Jamie and Roxy were settled in comfortably.

Mrs. Gibbons guided him to the guest wing of the house. "Those were delivered while you were gone," she said, indicating a single suitcase outside one door and two outside another. Motioning toward the door with the one suitcase beside it, she added, "Your son is in there. You and your wife have the other room. I had the men leave the suitcases outside so that Mrs. Bishop and your son would not be disturbed."

Eric thanked her, then, carrying Jamie's suitcase into the boy's room, he stood for a long moment watching him sleep. Fear for what could have happened to the child because of him brought a dark frown to his face. Satisfied the boy was resting comfortably, he left.

Entering the room he was to share with Roxy, he set their suitcases on the floor and stood looking at her lying in the bed. Silently he vowed that he'd get her and Jamie safely through this business then get out of their lives. To his chagrin, this vow brought with it a bitter taste of regret. Heading into their private bathroom, he even found himself considering finding a new line of work, one that would not put at risk any family he might have. He scowled at himself as he climbed into the shower. He wouldn't be happy doing anything else. Besides, he'd determined long ago that a family wasn't for him, and he was fairly certain that after tonight Roxy would wholeheartedly agree with him.

The moment she had those papers making Jamie legally hers, he'd bid her goodbye and get back to saving the world from the bad guys. The thought of being on his own once again and back to work was supposed to give him something to look forward to. Instead the bitter taste of regret lingered. "I'm just tired," he grumbled under his breath. "And sore," he added as he soaped over a bruise.

A few minutes later, trying not to disturb Roxy, he slipped quietly under the covers. Their remembered love-making had tempted him to wake her, but he guessed she wasn't interested in having anything to do with him at the moment. Maybe not ever again. Being shot at on their wedding night could dampen anyone's passion.

Roxy had woken when he'd first entered the room. It was as if, even in sleep, she'd been waiting for him. Knowing he had to be tired, she'd waited until he'd show-ered and was lying down. Now, unable to curb her curi-osity any longer, she turned toward him, levered herself on an elbow and asked, "What's going on?" Worry and nerves caused the words to come out harshly.

Noting the agitated edge in her voice, Eric assumed the anger he'd been expecting had finally surfaced. Well, he deserved it. Levelly, he said, "I thought you were asleep."

"I was, but I'm not now. I want to know what's going on." She repeated her request with firm determination.

He knew telling her what she wanted to know would only validate her fury, but he had no choice. He refused to lie to her or even hedge on the truth. "The man who came into our bedroom tonight is the same one who shot me three years ago. Apparently Tobias didn't clean up all the loose ends." He scowled with impatience. "I know something someone doesn't want me to remember. After I've gotten some sleep, Tobias wants to try some relaxa-tion techniques."

The self-recrimination in his voice tore at her. "You'll remember," she assured him.

Startled that she hadn't thrown a fistful of accusations at him, he looked hard into her face. In the daylight fil-tering in through the closed curtains, to his continued surprise he read only concern. "I really am sorry about dragging you and Jamie into this."

She wanted to be angry with him but couldn't. He hadn't drawn them into danger on purpose. Besides, if she and Jamie hadn't been there, he would probably be dead, and that was a thought that she couldn't bear. "You know what Maude always used to say…when life hands you a basket of lemons, make lemonade." She smiled crookedly. "In my case, I visualize lemon meringue pie."

"Thanks for being so understanding," he said gratefully. "And I promise you, you and Jamie will get out of this safely."

"I trust you." She hadn't realized until she'd spoken just how honest those words were. Then noticing the spreading bruising on his shoulder, she frowned. "You're hurt."

"Just a few bumps." The note of anxiety in her voice caused a curl of pleasure. *She'd show the same sympathy for any of us good guys,* he told himself dryly.

Roxy had had a long talk with herself this evening, most of which had been aimed at curbing her growing attachment to Eric. However, she argued, it was only humane to offer comfort. "I could kiss them and make them better," she volunteered.

"I've always wondered if that really worked or if it was just an old wives' tale," he replied, surprised by her offer. He'd been certain that in spite of her open-mindedness about having her life placed in danger, her desire for any intimacy with him had been dampened.

She kissed his shoulder gently and marveled at how good he tasted. "Does that feel better?"

Her lips caused a warmth to spread over the immediate area. "I believe so."

"Where else does it hurt?" she asked.

"Here." He pushed the covers away and pointed to a spot on his chest.

She kissed it, then circled kisses all around the first one. In spite of all that had happened during the past hours, being with him still seemed incredibly right. Or maybe her hormones, once awakened, were working overtime to make up for all those years she'd forced them into dormancy, she mused. Whatever the reason, the passion he'd aroused within her was burning as hot as ever.

"Clearly, physical contact with a nurturing female does have a soothing effect on pain," he said gruffly, wrapping his arms around her and drawing her closer.

"I'm glad to be of service." Trailing kisses upward, she found his lips.

Eric forgot his tiredness and his frustration at not being able to remember those months before the coma. All he could think about was the feel of her beneath his hands and the comforting heat contact with her body produced.

Again Roxy reminded herself that for Jamie's and her safety she should put distance between them and Eric Bishop as quickly as possible. But until that time came, she reasoned, she might as well enjoy herself. Forgetting everything but the delicious way he made her body sing, she gave in to the fires of desire burning hot within her.

Chapter Nine

Roxy woke as Eric left the bed. When he began to dress, she glanced toward the clock and frowned. "You only got a couple of hours' sleep."

"I've gotten by on less." Finishing zipping his slacks, he leveled his gaze on her. "I won't rest easy until I know you and Jamie are out of danger."

And that means being erased from your life once the bad guys are caught, she added silently, this thought causing her stomach to knot. She saw the lines of strain on his face and guessed he was looking forward to not having two albatrosses slung around his neck. Mentally she frowned at herself. She knew he didn't think of her and Jamie in such harsh terms. He thought of them as a good deed he'd tried to do and bungled. But she didn't doubt that the sooner he was rid of them, the better he would like it.

As he left the room, she found herself thinking that he was a good man and it was a shame he wasn't traveling a path she and Jamie could join him on. Abruptly her jaw tightened. There was no sense in wishful thinking. He'd chosen his path in life and she'd chosen hers. But even more important, he wasn't in love with her and he wasn't going to fall in love with her. "And I'm not in love with him, nor am I going to fall in love with him," she affirmed aloud, tossing off the covers and leaving the bed.

She opened the second suitcase, and her eyes rounded in surprise. Along with her clothes and a few toilet articles was the box holding her Tarot cards. Obviously Eric had mentioned to Tobias the cards and their importance to her. Aware that a great many people thought those people who believed in reading cards were odd, a flush began to build from her neck upward. "Well, everyone has their little idiosyncrasies," she muttered under her breath, and busied herself dressing.

Stopping by Jamie's room before going downstairs, she discovered it was empty. An open suitcase on his floor told her that he'd found his fresh clothes. Descending the stairs, she encountered a pretty, auburn-haired, green-eyed woman near her own age.

"You must be Roxy Bishop," the woman said, extending her hand in greeting. "I'm Hesper Lawton, Tobias's grandniece and his accountant."

"It's nice to meet you." Accepting the handshake, Roxy noted the open friendliness in the other's woman eyes. She was surprised by Hesper's easy acceptance of her, then realized that everyone had treated her and Jamie like welcome guests. Clearly, Tobias ran a hospitable household. "Have you seen a ten-year-old boy around?"

"Jamie. Yes." Hesper smiled. "Come along." Leading the way down a long hall, she said, "I hope you don't mind. We don't have much to interest children in this house, so I taught him how to play a game on the computer. He learned fast. He seems to have a knack for technology."

"I didn't know that. A seven-year-old television was the most modern thing we had on the farm," Roxy replied.

Jamie glanced up at her as she entered. His eyes were glistening. "Hesper said she'd teach me all about computers."

Roxy wanted to warn him not to plan on staying too long, but couldn't bring herself to diminish his joy. For the first time he was behaving like a ten-year-old. Well, not exactly, she corrected. Most ten-year-olds, raised in a lower middle class home, would have been intimidated by this house, but he seemed perfectly at ease. A second revelation stunned her. She felt secure and comfortable here, as well. *After nearly being murdered last night, any sanctuary would feel safe and welcoming,* she reasoned. Aloud she said, "We are in the midst of the computer age. One of us should learn something about them."

He nodded and returned to his game.

"You missed lunch," Hesper said. "I'll have Gretchen fix you something."

Jamie abruptly looked up at Roxy and grinned. "Gretchen is Tobias's cook. She's a little scary, but her bark's worse than her bite. At least, that's what Tobias told me."

Hesper gave the boy a comradely wink, then turned her attention back to Roxy. "How about a roast beef sandwich or, if you're a vegetarian, I believe there is some quiche left."

"I can get something for myself," Roxy replied, uneasy about being waited on.

Hesper grimaced apologetically. "Gretchen is very protective of her territory."

"A roast beef sandwich, then," Roxy conceded.

"Coffee? Soda? Juice? Mayonnaise? Tomato? Lettuce?" Hesper asked, picking up the phone and punching in a couple of digits.

"Mayonnaise, tomato, lettuce and coffee with milk."

Hesper placed the order. "It'll be served in the sitting room at the front of the house." Again acting as guide, she showed Roxy the way. At the door she stopped. "I'll leave you on your own. I have work to do."

"Thank you," Roxy said.

With a parting smile, Hesper left.

Entering the room, Roxy stood inspecting her surroundings. Furnished in Victorian style, the small room had a stately, old-world charm. A huge vase of roses filled the air with their soft fragrance and she found herself picturing ladies in turn-of-the-century gowns having tea.

"I furnished this room with my mother's things," Tobias said, joining her. "Since I've been a bachelor all of my life, this is the only room in the house with a truly feminine touch. I hope you find it relaxing. You have been through a great deal."

"It's lovely."

He smiled warmly. "I see your things found their way to you."

The flush that had begun earlier returned. "Yes, thank you."

"Please, sit." He motioned toward a chair. When Roxy obeyed, he seated himself on the love seat. "I hope you didn't think it was presumptuous of me to have your cards included."

Surprised he mentioned them, she looked for ridicule beneath his mask of politeness. There was none. Still, she felt uncomfortable admitting to someone she barely knew how much she looked to them for guidance. "No, of course not. In fact, I appreciate you having them brought to me. They're a sort of family heirloom. I feel more relaxed knowing they are safely with me.''

"They've been in your family a long time then?" Tobias's smile warmed even more. "Antiquities are a hobby of mine. Would you mind if I took a look at them?"

"They're not antiques. I consider them heirlooms because my great-grandmother made them for me."

"An original creation. How exciting."

"Not exactly original. She copied them from a deck her mother had." Immediately Roxy regretted having spoken. She was revealing far too much.

"Then it would be safe to say that the women in your family have consulted the Tarot for a number of generations." A polite plea showed on Tobias's face. "I hope you don't feel I'm being intrusive. The truth is that Eric mentioned that you read the cards and it piqued my interest. Have all of the women in your family been readers?"

"Not all of them." Certain he was simply patronizing her in an effort to make her feel more at home here, Roxy shifted uncomfortably.

Tobias's expression became more serious. "I've known some very important people who looked to readers and seers for advice."

Realizing that his interest was genuine, Roxy's embarrassment lessened a little.

"You must have talent," Tobias continued. "Eric is a skeptic and yet he heeded the warning your cards gave enough to mention it to me."

Roxy frowned. "I misread the immediacy of the danger."

"An old Gypsy once told me that the cards cannot be

used to predict the future. They can only give glimpses of what forces revolve around a person.''

She studied him narrowly. ''You have a much greater knowledge of this subject than most people.''

He shrugged. ''I've always been interested in anything dealing with man's sixth sense or, as the scientists like to term it, our extrasensory perception. And I would very much like to see your cards.''

The maid arrived at that moment with Roxy's lunch.

Tobias waited until she'd moved a table in front of Roxy and removed the food from the tray, setting it out properly, then he said, ''Please fetch the wooden box that came with Mrs. Bishop's things.''

''Yes, sir,'' the woman replied, and was gone.

''Eat,'' Tobias commanded Roxy.

The talk about the cards had made her nervous, causing her to forget her hunger. But with the food now in front of her, it returned. Without encouragement, she bit into the sandwich.

Leaning back in his chair, Tobias smiled thoughtfully. ''I'll tell you a secret, if you give me your word you won't repeat it.''

Curious, and thinking he was going to tell her something about Eric he felt Eric would not tell her on his own, she said, ''You have my word.''

''My great-great-grandmother claimed she could trace her family lineage all the way back to the ancient Druids. Now, there was a people who were supposed to have had strong ESP talents.''

Roxy managed to hide her surprise at this announcement. Reminding herself that he was in the business of detecting, it occurred to her that he'd had her investigated and discovered that her great-grandmother, who made money on the side reading cards, had claimed to be a descendant of the Druids. Roxy had always believed her great-grandmother had made the claim to drum up business, until her grandmother confided to her that the Druid heritage was real, and used their ability to read the cards as proof. Respect and love for Faye Swain had caused Roxy to allow the elderly woman the benefit of the doubt. However, she suspected that Tobias was simply leading her on, trying to determine if she was one brick short of a full load. "I was under the impression that the Druids had all been killed off."

"So the history books tell us. I, however, am always skeptical about what I read. I find it very difficult to believe that so talented a group of people could be entirely wiped out. It seems more likely to me that they escaped and hid themselves by assimilating into other cultures."

"I suppose that could have happened," she conceded noncommittally, and applied herself to her food.

The maid arrived soon after with the wooden box containing the cards. Roxy noted that he treated them with respect as he took them out and studied them closely. "They're beautiful," he said after a few minutes.

Roxy had been forcing herself to eat calmly as if his handling them was of no significance. Inwardly, she was pleased that he was placing his imprint on them. The first chance she got, she would read them and see what they revealed about him.

As if he'd read her mind, Tobias extended the deck toward her. "Will you read them for me?"

Unable to resist finding out if he was playing games with her or was serious about all he'd said, she took the cards and laid them out. The array revealed a man of deep strengths. Aloud she said, "You feel strongly about family, loyalty and honesty. There is also an aura of mystery and intrigue surrounding you. Danger lurks in the shadows, but you're well protected. You have a great deal of power. You're also a man I should trust.''

''I hope you will keep that last in mind should you ever require aid,'' Tobias said. Then, thanking her, he left.

For a long time she sat looking at the array. It would be easy to attribute the mystery and intrigue to his line of work. But her gut instinct was that it went deeper into the essence of the man himself.

''Of course, my gut instinct wasn't so accurate where Eric was concerned,'' she reminded herself. But was that really true? Or had she ignored the intensity of the warnings that the danger surrounding him was due to an immediate threat because down deep she'd wanted to? ''I had no choice. I needed his help,'' she growled under her breath. Besides, there had been the triad. Of course, she'd misinterpreted that, too. It hadn't signified protection for Jamie, but for Eric. Even so, she could not be angry with herself for any of her decisions. A great deal of good had grown out of them. However, she promised herself, in the future she would be more conservative in her behavior.

Leaving the sitting room, she went up to her bedroom to put the cards away. Eric was there splashing cold water on his face.

''You look exhausted,'' she said when he finished toweling dry and she saw the dark circles under his eyes and the lines of strain on his face.

''I've been trying to remember using relaxation techniques,'' he replied.

''You look more like you've been in battle.''

He grimaced. ''I was trying too hard. Hagen told me to take a break.''

The mention of her family to Tobias had caused a new worry to nag at her. ''I need to contact my parents and tell them what happened and that I'm all right before they hear it from someone else.''

"Call them, but keep the conversation under two minutes," he instructed. "Their line might be bugged. I'm pretty sure whoever is after me has guessed I'm here, but there's no reason to let him know for certain.''

She nodded and dialed the number while he stretched out on the bed.

Hanging up after a very quick, cryptic phone call, she considered lying down beside him. The urge was great...so great that alarms went off in her head. She was growing much too fond of his company. "I'd better go check on Jamie," she said.

Eric had been considering encouraging her to join him, but having her in his bed was not conducive to remembering the past, and that was his number-one priority at the moment. Too restless to remain alone, he rose. "I'll go with you."

Downstairs they found Jamie browsing through the computer's menu. "There's great stuff on here," he said, taking his eyes off the screen for only a second to acknowledge their presence.

Eric and Roxy watched for a few minutes, then, leaving Jamie to his exploring, they left. Out in the hall Roxy glanced back and frowned with motherly concern. "Do you think Tobias might have a baseball or basketball lying around? I think I should see that Jamie gets some physical exercise as well as mental."

"Hagen informed me that the building on the other side of the patio houses a fully stocked gym and an indoor swimming pool. We're welcome to use them whenever we wish," Eric replied.

"Good. I'm glad Jamie's enjoying the computer, but I don't want him turning into one of those pale indoor types who spend their life on the Internet and rarely socialize with anyone who isn't a computer jockey like themselves."

An image suddenly began to take shape in Eric's mind. Instead of quickly fading out before he could grasp it fully, it grew stronger and more complete. Turning Roxy into his arms, he gave her a hug. "Thanks to you and Jamie, I may have begun to remember something important."

Locked in his grateful embrace, Roxy experienced a rush of joy. Even after he released her and strode away, her heart continued to pound with excitement. She'd helped him, and the amount of pleasure that gave her was astonishing.

She and Jamie had helped him, her inner voice corrected. The triad came sharply into her mind. "Don't even start thinking about the three of you staying together," she admonished herself.

"Would talking to someone other than yourself help with whatever is worrying you?" a female voice asked.

Roxy turned to see Hesper in the doorway of a nearby room. "I was just thinking that being married to one of Tobias's operatives would be hard on family life. You'd always be worried they were in danger," she answered honestly.

"It's something you learn to live with."

A knowing edge in the woman's voice caused Roxy to study her more closely. Seeing the wedding ring on Hesper's finger, she asked, "Does your husband work for Tobias?"

"Yes. And you're right, his job is a strain on my nerves. But I love him. I can't imagine life without him."

"That better be me you're talking about," a tall, dark-haired man said, striding toward them.

Hesper's eyes sparkled. "I was just on my way to meet you." Clearly forgetting everything except the man, she raced into his arms.

As they kissed, Roxy could see that they were very much in love. And if Eric loved her... She stopped the thought. He didn't and she wouldn't even let herself consider the possibility. If she did, she might start thinking that the strong physical attraction she felt for him went deeper, and that would only cause her greater hurt when they parted company.

While Roxy was witnessing Garth Lawton's homecoming, Eric had found Tobias. "I've remembered something," he said. "It might be nothing, but it ties in with computer whizzes."

Tobias buzzed for Hagen. "Let's hear it," he said as soon as Hagen joined them.

"After I faked my own death, Susan came out to California to make personal contact with me and set up a communication code system no one would suspect or catch on to. I was to meet her at a small café in Los Angeles, the kind with outside tables. Since I had plenty of time on my hands, and having been told by her that this assignment was of the highest priority, I arrived two hours early and staked the place out. She arrived just a couple of minutes later and sat down at one of the outside tables. Because she was there so early, I thought maybe I had the time wrong. I was on my way to join her when this guy showed up. He had a computer case slung on his shoulder, thick glasses and one of those plastic pen holders in his shirt pocket crammed full of pencils and pens. His shirt was buttoned crooked and his pants were a size too big. His sneakers were worn and he'd wound gray electrician's tape around one of them to hold it together.

He was the perfect stereotypical nerd...almost too perfect, now that I think about it."

"Can you give me a more complete description of the man himself?" Tobias asked.

"Six feet tall, maybe an inch more, slender, clean shaven, strong jawline, angular features, thick blond hair worn long in a ponytail."

Tobias nodded impatiently. "He doesn't sound familiar. We'll do an artist's sketch. What happened next?"

"She looked amused when he approached her table. I was surprised when she let him sit down, but I figured she'd decided that he'd be good entertainment while she waited for me. She always did have an unusual sense of humor. But I didn't like the two of us hanging around the same place too long. I caught her eye as I started toward her table. She smiled and waved. The guy frowned like he'd thought he was making a conquest and suddenly realized he wasn't. He glared at me, got up so fast he nearly knocked over his chair and stalked off. At the time I assumed he was worried about being confronted by a jealous boyfriend. But it could have been that he didn't want me getting a long look at him. Susan joked about him trying to pick her up using lines like, 'I'll bet we could do some great computing together' and 'Would you like to come up to my place to see my mainframe?' Then we discussed business and parted company. I never gave the guy a second thought until now."

"And now you think he might be our Mr. CW?" Tobias asked.

"It's possible. They could have figured they'd have plenty of time to meet before I showed up. Susan wouldn't have expected me to be there two hours early."

"Sounds plausible," Tobias agreed. He turned to Hagen. "Time to try out that new computer program and see if we can get a reasonable composite of our nerd."

As they began to work, Eric frowned. "Something's wrong. The glasses were thick and yet I saw his eyes as if I was looking through a clear window."

"Fake glasses?" Hagen suggested.

Eric nodded. "And if they were fake, then the whole look could have been fake. Like I said before, he was almost too stereotypical. A disguise would also explain the amused look on Susan's face."

"A disguise would be in keeping with the cautious nature of our Mr. CW," Tobias conceded.

"So we get rid of the glasses and maybe even the long hair and concentrate on the jawline and facial features," Hagen said.

"Right," Eric agreed.

A couple of hours later Eric went in search of Roxy and Jamie. He found them playing a game on the computer.

"Did you remember whatever it was you needed to remember?" Roxy asked, guessing the answer by the more relaxed expression on his face.

"My gut instinct says so," he replied. "Tobias has sent a sketch out to people he trusts. Until we hear anything, I'm to relax and enjoy myself. So I thought that if the two of you could pull yourselves away from the computer, we'd have a picnic dinner down by the lake. Hagen says it's about half a mile beyond the back garden."

"Could we go fishing?" Jamie asked hopefully. "Roxy and I used to fish in the evening when all our chores were done."

"Your wish is my command," Eric replied.

With their basket of food retrieved from the kitchen and

fishing equipment gathered from the store Tobias kept for visitors, Eric and Roxy strolled down the wide path leading to the lake. Jamie ran in front of them, pausing periodically to inspect some interesting insect or plant while waiting for them to catch up. The lake, while small as lakes went, was one of the prettiest she'd ever seen, Roxy thought as they drew near their destination. Its irregular perimeter fingered into small coves created by the mountainous terrain. For his guests' comfort and easy access to the water, Tobias had cleared a section of trees and built a pier. He'd also had a rough path cut along a portion of the bank. But for the most part, the Vermont forest surrounding the water had been left untouched.

Roxy spread the blanket on the grassy bank just beyond the pier and began to unpack the food while Jamie and Eric rigged the fishing lines and chose their lures.

Jamie ate hurriedly, then, taking his rod and a net, scampered down to the pier.

"This was really nice of you," Roxy said as she and Eric watched the boy cast.

Eric smiled. "Figured I owed you two some fun. Last night was a pretty harrowing experience."

"You're the only one who is the worse for wear," she replied.

The concern in her eyes warmed him. This, he thought, looking from her to Jamie, was what he'd fantasized having a family would be like.

"It's so peaceful. Reminds me of evenings at the farm," Roxy said.

"That was the first place I ever lived where I felt as if I was truly wanted." Abruptly, Eric's jaw tensed. But even that hadn't lasted. Again he recalled the disappointment he'd felt the first and only time he'd returned, to discover his time there was over. He'd never place himself in the position of facing that kind of disappointment again. Roxy and Jamie would never really be ''his'' family. He'd just been invited along as a necessary acquaintance for the moment.

Roxy saw his expression harden. ''I guess you had a pretty rough childhood.''

He shrugged as if to say that was unimportant. ''Every life has its rough spots.'' He grimaced. ''I seem to have provided one of those for you and Jamie. As soon as I'm sure you're both safe, I'll take a hike.''

Roxy experienced a jab of regret. Don't be an idiot, she scolded herself. He'd never planned to stay in the first place and, in the second, she didn't want a husband whose life she was constantly fearing for. Still, the regret lingered. Determined to think only of the moment, she lay back and watched the clouds drifting over the tops of the mountains. ''At least you provided us with a lovely spot to wait out this trouble.''

Eric mentally patted himself on the back. Her easy acceptance of him getting out of her life made it clear she had no desire for their relationship to be a lasting one. And neither did he, he added, again reminding himself that he'd already determined that a wife and family would interfere with his chosen path. ''A lovely spot,'' he agreed.

Roxy suddenly sat up. In the next instant she was on her feet heading to the pier. Seeing Jamie calmly fishing, she came to an abrupt halt.

''What's wrong?'' Eric demanded, hurrying to her side.

''Didn't you hear the child crying?'' she demanded. The sobbing had stopped before she'd gone even two steps. Still she continued to peer into the woods and across the lake, seeking the source of the anguished weeping.

"No." Seeing the panic on her face and wanting to help ease her mind, he said, "Maybe you dozed off momentarily and dreamed it."

Roxy drew a calming breath. "I suppose that could have happened," she conceded. Still, it had been so vivid. "Jamie," she called down to the pier, "did you hear anything just now that sounded like a child crying?"

He paused in the midst of a cast. "No."

She heard the concern in his voice. When he started up the pier, she waved him to stop. "It was nothing. Go on with your fishing."

He nodded and obeyed.

For a long moment she continued to stand staring out over the water. She had Jamie with her. That was supposed to stop the crying that had haunted her. But this crying wasn't the same. This time she'd been certain it was a little girl. She scowled at herself. It was impossible to be certain of the gender of a child by the sound of its sobbing. "You're right. I must have dozed off and had a short nightmare," she said, more to herself than to Eric.

She's still haunted by the child she lost, he reasoned. Empathy for her pain swept through him. It was followed by a strong desire to protect her and ease her hurt. He placed a comradely arm around her shoulders. "How about if we join Jamie?"

Roxy nodded. Pushing the sobbing from her mind, she turned her full attention to fishing.

Eric was netting Jamie's third fish when Hagen joined them. "Gretchen said she'd cook up whatever we caught for breakfast," the boy said excitedly. "Would you like me to catch one for you?"

Hagen smiled. "Some other time." His smile became an expression of apology. "Eric will have to take a rain check, as well."

"Does Tobias have a lead on our man?" Eric asked, his manner suddenly all business as he handed the netted fish over to Roxy and straightened to face Hagen.

"No. But there's a computer show in California. Los Angeles, to be exact. A big one. Tobias suspects our man might show up there. He wants us there. You look for our man while Garth and I guard your back."

Jamie slipped his hand into Eric's. "You'll need me and Roxy. We're a team."

"Not this time." Eric ruffled the boy's hair. "This time I need the two of you to stay here where you're safe."

"We want to go," Jamie insisted, his hold on Eric tightening.

Roxy was shaken by how strong the boy's attachment to the man had become. She was even more shocked by her own wish to go along. But this time her intuition told her that wish was irrational and she realized it had come from a tremendous surge of protectiveness toward her husband. "Eric doesn't need us there to worry about," she soothed. "He needs to be able to concentrate on catching the bad guys."

"And he'll be in disguise," Hagen added. "Even you wouldn't recognize him, and I'll never take my eyes off him."

The child's concern touched Eric deeply. *Don't go getting mushy*, he ordered himself. *The boy goes with Roxy*. Working his hand free, he bent over until his face was level with Jamie's. "I'm counting on you to take care of Roxy until I get back."

"I will," the boy promised, clearly pleased to have a duty.

"See you both soon," Eric said as he straightened.

Roxy merely nodded, her fear for him having increased to a point that made speaking impossible. But as he headed to the house with Hagen, she knew she couldn't let him go without having said something. Racing up the path after him, she caught up with him and Hagen at the edge of the lawn.

"I'll see you at the house," Hagen said, continuing on so that they could have a moment alone.

"I just wanted to tell you to be careful," Roxy said in answer to the question on Eric's face.

"I'm always careful," he assured her, liking the concern he saw in her eyes.

"When you said you led a dangerous life, I never realized just how frightening that could be," she heard herself confessing.

The pleasure her concern had brought turned cold. He didn't like worrying her this way. "I know what I'm doing."

"You probably thought you knew what you were doing when you got shot." The thought had been blurted out, her fear for him breaking her control.

He frowned impatiently. "That was different. I didn't have friends to back me up."

Her cheeks flushed with embarrassment. Trying to cover up the depth of emotion her outburst had exposed, she said hurriedly, "I'm sorry. I sound like a nag. It's just that this whole business has my nerves on edge."

He kissed her lightly on the nose. "I'll be back soon and in one piece." What she'd sounded like was a wife, he thought as he continued on to the house. But the thought brought no pleasure. Even if she was developing feelings for him, it wouldn't be fair to put a person through the kind of worry a woman married to him would have to endure. He was also pretty sure no woman would put up with it forever. Just when he let himself get used to coming home to someone, he'd probably find a note saying she couldn't take it any longer and had found a man with a more regular job.

As he walked away, Roxy held back the tears of fear burning at the back of her eyes. This was definitely not the kind of home environment she wanted for herself or for Jamie. The sooner they parted company with Eric Bishop, the better. But even as she told herself this, a sharp jab of pain pierced her.

"I shouldn't let the fact that he's great in bed blur my thinking," she grumbled at herself, refusing to admit just how deeply she'd learned to care for him.

Chapter Ten

Roxy lay for a long time staring into the dark. She'd had a hard time going to sleep. The bed had felt lonely without Eric. She'd tried telling herself that she was simply worried for his safety. The truth, she was finally forced to admit, was that she missed him horribly. Following this admission, she'd reminded herself for the umpteenth time that their arrangement was not a permanent one. Instead of helping, that had made her feel even worse.

Grudgingly, she'd confessed to her growing feelings for him but insisted that they were due to her fear that she'd never be able to find another man who would disregard her scarring and her inability to have children. Finally, assuring herself that although she liked Eric Bishop a lot, she wasn't in love with him, she'd fallen asleep.

Now she was awake again. Her body was trembling and there were tears in her eyes. It was a dream that had woken her...a very vivid dream about a little girl. The child was standing in front of two graves, sobbing uncontrollably and holding her arms out to Roxy for comfort.

What was even more disconcerting was that there was something familiar about this experience.

Roxy raked her fingers through her hair. Her imagination was simply working overtime, she told herself and ordered herself back to sleep.

Again she dozed and again she was awakened by the crying child. Climbing out of bed, she found her cards and laid them out. The array was very like the one that had signaled Jamie coming into her life. Fear swept through her. What was happening to her?

Unable to remain in the confines of her room, she dressed and went downstairs. The sitting room where she'd had her chat with Tobias beckoned. Entering it, she used the light of the moon streaming in the windows to find her way to a chair. There she sat, staring out at the shadowy landscape beyond the glass panes. Her body was taut and her hands were trembling. She realized she was waiting, listening for the child's sobbing to begin again.

"Is something wrong?" Tobias's voice broke into her thoughts.

She glanced toward the door to see him, dressed in a robe over pajamas, making his way toward her. Feeling guilty for having woken him, she said, "I'm sorry. I didn't mean to disturb you."

"To be honest, I rarely sleep more than a couple of hours at a time. I'm not sure if it's age or if, because of the business I'm in, I've learned to survive on naps." He'd left the lights off as he made his way across the room and took a chair near hers. "If you're worried about Eric, I can assure you that he is well guarded."

"I am worried about him," she admitted. Suddenly the child's sobbing filled the room. Roxy's hold on the arm of the chair tightened until her knuckles were white. "Do you hear anything?" she demanded.

"Define *anything*," Tobias requested.

For a moment Roxy hesitated, then said stiffly, "A child crying."

"No."

Tears of panic trickled down her cheeks. "I do. I've been hearing it since early this evening. I don't understand what's happening to me."

Tobias patted her hand. "I'm sure there's a reasonable explanation."

Roxy brushed the tears away. "I wish there was."

"You strike me as a young woman with both feet planted firmly on the ground," he said encouragingly.

"Even though I read Tarot cards?"

"I told you that I have an open mind about such things."

Roxy knew she had to talk to someone. Even if she could call her parents or her grandmother and talk as long as she wanted, she couldn't tell them what was happening. They would worry that she was losing her mind, and she didn't want to put them through that kind of suffering. Besides, she was worried enough for all of them. *Looks like Tobias wins by default,* she mused. "You also told me that your family claims to have descended from the Druids. My great-grandmother told me the same thing. She said that was why we could read the cards. It was our inherited sixth sense."

"And you think that this heritage is the reason you're hearing a child crying?" Tobias prodded when she paused.

Roxy shook her head. "I don't know. When I was six months pregnant I was in a train wreck and lost my baby and the ability to ever have any more. My husband rejected me and I went through a rough time. I began to dream of a child crying out to me. My parents and my grandmother were certain the dreams were caused by depression. My grandmother decided that working with children would help me, so she sent me to Maude. The dreams continued until Jamie was brought to the farm. When he was taken away, they began again, only this time he was the child in them and I knew he needed me." Roxy paused and drew a terse breath. "I was certain the dreams were all bound to my need to replace the child I'd lost."

"And now you're not so certain?" Tobias asked.

"I have Jamie. That should have taken care of that need." Her chin trembled. "But now it's happening all over again. Only this time I've already seen the child who's sobbing. She's standing in front of two graves, and I can even read the information on the gravestones. They say Grace and Sam Carlson." She gave their birthdates, then added, "They both died recently...on the same day. August twelfth."

"August 12 would have been five days ago," Tobias noted.

Roxy looked pleadingly at him. "I don't understand why I'd dream any of that. I don't know any people by those names."

"Could you have heard a report on the radio or television involving the Carlsons? Maybe you read about them in the newspaper?"

Roxy shook her head. "I don't think so. Maybe, I guess. No. I really think I would remember reading the story if it made such a strong impression on me that I'd dream about the people involved. Besides, they don't usually give birth dates, do they?"

"No." Tobias switched on a lamp and found a pad of paper and a pencil. "Before you decide you're going mad, why don't I check and see if these people existed."

Her eyes rounded in surprise. "You actually think they could be real?"

"Jamie was real," he said matter-of-factly. "And you obviously have a very strong nurturing nature. Perhaps the sixth sense you inherited has been made stronger by your own adversity so that now it allows you to detect children who have some sort of link with your own heritage and are going through an emotional trauma from which they need you to rescue them."

"Do you know how bizarre that sounds?" she said.

"I've lived a long time," he replied in a fatherly voice. "And I've learned, as I've told you twice already, to have an open mind."

"I suppose finding out that I have a knack for discovering children who need me would be preferable to finding out I'm losing my mind."

Tobias asked her to repeat the names and dates so that he could jot them down. Then, smiling reassuringly, he rose. "I'll look into the matter personally. Now, I suggest you go back to bed and try to get some rest."

As she returned to her room, the thought that he was humoring her until Eric returned or until he could safely contact her family occurred to her. A sudden fear that she could lose Jamie shook her to the core. But if she was crazy, Jamie would be better off without her. Besides, Tobias had seemed sincere in his belief that she was not nuts.

Or maybe he's as loony as I am, she mused.

In his study, Tobias sat at the computer. Excitement glistened in his eyes. "It would appear that I was right about Roxanne Dugan. She is a unique woman." Then, jotting down an address, he turned off the machine and went back to bed.

* * *

Roxy awoke the next morning with the image of the young girl sitting in a chair waiting patiently lingering in her mind. "At least she's stopped crying," she muttered.

In the cold light of dawn she was embarrassed that she'd confided in Tobias. The most reasonable explanation for her imaginings was that she still had not dealt fully with the death of her child. But why she'd be hearing a girl was a puzzle. The child she'd lost had been a boy. That had been why thinking she could hear Jamie had seemed sort of natural. "Well, maybe not natural, but at least reasonable," she corrected.

However, telling Tobias had been useful to some extent, she told herself, trying to find a bright side. It had quelled her imagination somewhat. The child wasn't sobbing frantically any longer, and if the image didn't go away entirely, she'd seek help.

A knock sounded on her door. "The cook is frying the fish." Jamie's voice came through the barrier.

"I'll be right out," she called back.

Downstairs she discovered that Tobias was joining them for breakfast. A flush of embarrassment began to build from her neck upward. He smiled reassuringly and she wondered if he had men with a straitjacket waiting for her just beyond the door. If he did, he didn't call them in. He also didn't bring up their late-night conversation during the meal. Instead, he complimented Jamie on his fishing skill and centered the conversation on the boy, asking him how he liked school and what sports interested him.

Jamie, she noticed, talked freely to Tobias. And so had she. In her case, too freely, she berated herself.

Finishing eating and still beaming with the pride of one who had provided the food being consumed, Jamie rose.

"I'm going to go play on the computer for a while," he announced.

"I'll come with you," Roxy said, rising also.

"I'd like a moment of your time," Tobias requested, motioning for her to be seated once again.

"I'll catch up with you," she told Jamie, slowly sinking into her chair. *As long as Tobias doesn't have a paddy wagon waiting outside to take me to the nearest asylum.*

Jamie nodded and hurried on his way.

"I checked on those names and dates you gave me," Tobias said when they were alone. "Both were accurate."

A nervous tremor swept through her. "I'm not sure whether to be relieved or afraid." She studied him anxiously. "What about the little girl?"

"I'm having someone check on her. I'll let you know what we find out. In the meantime, try to relax. You obviously aren't delusional."

"I guess not," Roxy conceded. "But that doesn't make this feel any less eerie."

"Are you still hearing the sobbing?" he asked sympathetically.

"No. In the dream I was having just before I woke, I saw her sitting in a chair and had the impression she was waiting for me."

Tobias nodded. "We'll soon know."

As Roxy rose to leave, Eric's image came sharply into her mind. "Have you heard from Eric and the others?" she asked.

"They arrived in California safely." He glanced at his watch. "In a few hours they'll be going to the computer fair." He smiled reassuringly. "Eric will be disguised and his back well guarded."

She recalled the two men with guns who had broken

into the farm and a shiver of fear raced through her. "I hope so."

Out in the hall she discovered Hesper arriving for work. The worried look on the woman's face told her that Hesper was as concerned about her husband as Roxy was about Eric. "I don't know how you cope with being married to a man with such a dangerous occupation," she said, falling into step beside the accountant.

"If you love someone enough, you learn to accept their chosen paths," Hesper replied. She paused to study Roxy. "Didn't you know what Eric did for a living?"

"I knew he lived a dangerous life."

"They'll be fine," Hesper said with conviction, then hurried on to her office.

"I wish I could be as certain of that as she and Tobias are," Roxy muttered, wishing Eric would call so she could hear his voice. *You're thinking like a woman in love,* her inner voice scolded. *I'm just concerned,* she rebutted, but it felt like a lie. *This is no time to be falling in love,* she admonished curtly. She had enough on her mind. She didn't need any more complications.

Still, as the morning dragged on she couldn't stop thinking about Eric.

Jamie was concerned, as well. Every once in a while he'd turn to her and say, "Eric will be just fine, won't he?"

With a conviction she didn't feel, she always answered with a firm "Yes."

With his hair dyed black, a fake pot belly, glasses and a scar on his cheek, wearing jeans, a T-shirt that read Hackers Rule and a well-worn corduroy jacket, Eric Bishop entered the large auditorium with Hagen at his side and Garth in the rear. He'd recognized Garth Lawton from his days with The Unit and knew the man was one of the best.

But it wasn't his own back Eric was worried about. Roxy's and Jamie's faces filled his inner vision. It was their safety that mattered to him. Anger toward the man who had planned to kill him and Roxy and blame Jamie boiled within him. He'd get the coldhearted bastard if it was the last thing he did.

The show was gigantic, with every major company as well as most of the minor ones and entrepreneurs showing off their new hardware and software. For the next two hours Eric wandered among the booths.

"It's like looking for a needle in a haystack," he grumbled to Hagen in frustration.

"Let's get some coffee," Hagen suggested.

Eric nodded. A few minutes later they were seated at one of the small tables scanning the passersby.

"Have you found out about the two no-shows?" Hagen said quietly, his question directed to the small microphone in the lapel of his jacket.

"One company just went bankrupt. The other will be setting up late because they had a problem with their software," Garth replied through the small microphone in Hagen's ear.

"Anything?" Eric asked.

Hagen shook his head.

"Did you get a load of the fox Harvey found to man his booth?" one of the men at the next table asked his companions, his voice an exaggerated leer. "And she actually knows her stuff. Where do you think he found her?"

"I found her at the college," a man just joining the group said.

"One of the prof's students?" another man asked.

"He knows how to pick 'em and he knows how to teach 'em," Harvey replied. "I've had more play at my booth this year than the last two combined."

"I guess he'll be coming by later," one of the other men said. "I wanted to ask him about a software problem I've been having."

Harvey shook his head. "Gayle, that's the fox, says he has the flu and can't make it this year."

"Damn!" the man hoping to connect with the prof grumbled. "The guy's a genius." A bemused expression came over his face. "What I don't understand is why he isn't working for one of the major companies instead of teaching at an obscure technical college."

"He likes to do his own thing. A real independent sort," Harvey replied. "Besides, he doesn't need to work. He inherited money and just teaches because he likes the chicks. He told me so when I asked him how he could afford that Jaguar he drives on a teacher's salary."

Hagen looked to Eric with a question in his eyes.

"It can't hurt to check out this prof," Eric said. "If he isn't the man we're looking for, he might recognize him. If not, we can come back here and continue browsing."

Rising, Hagen lightly bumped into the man seated behind him at the next table. "Sorry," he apologized. His face lit up with recognition. "Harvey, isn't it?" He addressed the newest member of the group. "We met at a trade show last year." He extended his hand. "Name's Johnson."

"Yeah, sure." Harvey rose and accepted the handshake. It was obvious he had no clue who Hagen was, but like any good businessman, he refused to admit it.

"I just got here. I'm a little pressed for time," Hagen said. "But I don't want to miss your booth. Which one is it?"

"Number eighty-nine." Harvey's smile broadened. "I think you'll be impressed."

Hagen smiled back. "I'm sure I will."

A couple of minutes later he and Eric were standing in front of booth number eighty-nine. The shapely brunette seated at the computer in front of them was wearing a T-shirt, one size too small, with the logo of a local technical college stretched across her breasts.

"I heard you're a student of Professor..." Eric paused as if he couldn't remember the name. "The guy everyone says is such a genius with computers."

The girl smiled. "Professor Seaton."

Eric pushed his glasses up off the bridge of his nose. "Yes, that's the guy."

Hagen read the name of the school aloud for Garth's ears. "So that's where you learned how to manipulate those keys," he said with a playful leer.

Seeing where his gaze was focused, she frowned. "The hardware is just for show. But if you're interested in some great software, I can demonstrate what our company can offer."

"Some other time," Hagen replied.

She shrugged and turned her smile on the next possible customer.

"Meet you outside," Garth said in Hagen's ear. "I'm calling for the address and directions to the school right now."

A short while later they were making their way to the administration building on the campus of the technical college.

"Very convenient," Hagen said as they entered and saw an enclosed bulletin board with head shots of the college faculty and their names beneath.

The glasses were missing and the hair was cut in a

short, conservative style, but Eric had no trouble identifying their man. "Seaton's the one we're after," he said.

Hagen nodded toward the door. "Let's get out of here before he guesses he's been tagged."

Eric stood firm. "I won't allow Roxy and Jamie to remain in danger. I want him to know I remember him and I've told others. And I want him to know that if he harms one hair on either of their heads, he'll answer to me." He glowered with hatred at the photo on the wall. "Besides, I owe him a well-placed punch. He tried to kill Roxy."

Hagen caught his arm. "Putting this guy behind bars is the best way to protect your family."

Your family. The words rang in Eric's ears. They weren't his family, he reminded himself. They wanted a normal existence. Not the kind he would offer them.

"Roxy and Jamie are safe at Tobias's place," Garth added. "Besides, I figure it'll be twenty-four hours or less before Seaton knows you've tapped him. If this guy is as good a tech as people say he is, he'll be wired into any public access information systems and probably most of the private ones, as well. As soon as Tobias starts accessing files on him, he'll know."

Eric knew giving Tobias a head start on this guy was the right thing to do. Still, he wanted to take a punch at Seaton. "I want to be there when he's brought down," he growled.

"You will," Hagen promised.

A female student suddenly burst through the front doors, tears streaming down her cheeks.

"Professor Seaton's been killed," she blurted out, continuing down the hall and turning into one of the offices.

The men looked at one another, then quickly followed. At the door of the office they stopped. Inside, the girl was being comforted by another student, while two older women looked on in shock.

"I just heard it on the radio when I was driving in. It happened sometime last night. He went off that hairpin curve near his place, crashed on the beach and burned. Gayle always said he drove too fast," the student who had passed them in the hall choked out between sobs.

Eric looked to Hagen and Garth. In the next instant all three were on their way to their car. A call to Tobias got them the address of the morgue where the body had been taken and the name of the detective handling the case.

"The body was badly damaged by the fire and the crash," the pathologist informed them. "For the preliminary identification, I went by the physical description on Seaton's driver's license—height, weight—and the fact that the car was registered to him. This morning one of his neighbors identified the ring and watch we found on the corpse as his. I'm supposed to be getting his dental records later today or tomorrow and that should clinch the ID."

As they left the morgue to seek out the detective in charge of the case, Eric glanced at his two companions. "Do you think the remains they have are really his?"

"The timing was a little too coincidental for my taste," Garth replied, and Hagen nodded in agreement. "My guess is that he managed to hack into some of the supposedly secure lines Tobias was using to send the sketch you two came up with and decided it was time to cut and run. If he was anywhere near as clever as people say, he'd have a plan of escape."

"Just what I was thinking myself," Eric said.

They found Detective Green at his desk. "Scanlon, Lawton and Bishop?" he asked as they approached.

Hagen nodded, smiled politely and held out his hand. "Detective Green?"

His manner cordial, Green rose and accepted the handshake. "I just got a call asking me to cooperate with you guys. You're interested in the Seaton death? You think it could have been something other than a simple accident?"

"We really don't know. We were hoping we could take a look at your report and then nose around his place," Hagen said, taking the role of spokesman while Garth and Eric positioned themselves a little behind him.

"You know something about him I should know?" Green asked.

"We suspect he might be someone we've been looking for," Hagen replied.

"You Feds?"

Hagen shrugged noncommittally.

"Okay, forget I asked." Green smiled wryly. "I was told not to be inquisitive, but it's in my nature."

"We're just checking to see if he's the right guy," Hagen said in friendly tones, clearly not wanting to make Detective Green feel as if his turf was being trampled.

Green regarded them all suspiciously for a long moment, then shrugged. "I've got a deskful of work. If you guys want this one, you've got it."

"We'd just like to take a look at your report and nose around his place." Hagen repeated his original request. "We didn't come here to step on your toes."

The hint of defiance in Green's manner vanished. "My report's sketchy as yet," he said, handing Hagen the folder. "As for looking around his place, I couldn't find any next of kin, so I guess there's no one to object."

Hagen handed the report to Eric, then fell into step beside Green who was already heading to the exit.

On the way out to Seaton's place, Eric glanced through

what Green had. "Says here that there was a suitcase in the trunk."

"Yeah, figured he was going on a trip," Green replied. "Must have been in a rush. Probably late for a plane and drove himself off the cliff. People do stupid things when they feel pushed for time." He chuckled. "Take my wife. Every time she's in a rush, she locks her keys in her car."

Eric had to admit that Seaton could have panicked, but his gut instinct argued against it. From what they were learning of the man, he was cold, calculating and confident of his ability to handle any situation.

"Nice place," Hagen remarked as they parked in front of the beach house that had been Seaton's residence.

Green nodded. "His neighbors told me he inherited money. He'd have had to. No one could afford this kind of beachfront property on a teacher's salary."

"Expensive?" Hagen asked.

"Expensive and then some."

Inside, they found the place in immaculate order. Entering the study, Hagen sat down at the computer and began to access files, while Garth and Eric started through the desk drawers and filing cabinets.

Standing out of the way, Green watched them with interest. "Anytime you guys want to share, I'd be happy to listen."

Obviously deciding that the man's entire cooperation was worth revealing some information, Hagen said, "We're looking for a man who deals in munitions thefts and drugs."

The pleasure of one brought into the inner circle showed on Green's face. "And you think this Seaton was your man?"

"Maybe," Hagen returned.

"I'd say more than a maybe." Garth swung the door

of the room closed. On the back was a dart board with the sketch Tobias had faxed to his connections in the FBI and Interpol. It was covered with dart holes and three darts remained in it. "Looks like we guessed right about him finding out we were closing in on him."

"So he panicked, packed a suitcase and took off down the road at a breakneck speed that sent him over the cliff," Green mused.

"Looks that way," Hagen replied.

A little later, after having dropped Detective Green off at the police station, Eric cast a skeptical glance at his two companions. "You don't really believe that was Seaton in that car, do you?"

Hagen shook his head. "My bet is that it wasn't. The death was just too convenient. He's probably had some poor patsy lined up for a long time. I'll bet a month's salary that even the dental records confirm that it was Seaton in that car. But we'll let him think we bought his ploy. He might get cocky and make a mistake."

"Guess you're relieved," Garth said, grinning in a comradely way at Eric. "Even if he's still alive, killing you won't serve any purpose now, so you're off the hook."

"Yeah, off the hook," Eric repeated. It was over. There was still the adoption, but he knew Tobias had enough friends in high places that the papers would go through without a hitch and without his physical presence in Roxy's and Jamie's lives. They could go back to the farm and back to their previous existence and he could remain with Tobias and get back to catching the bad guys. The bitter taste of regret filled his mouth and he was forced to admit that he'd miss them.

The thought that he could get a job with the local police in Zephyr occurred to him, but writing speeding tickets wasn't his style. He'd be miserable, and in the end he'd make Roxy and Jamie miserable. He smiled wryly to himself. Besides, what made him think Roxy would even consider a life with him? She'd made it clear their relationship was strictly short-term, and even though he knew she enjoyed his company in her bed, she'd continued to let him know she didn't plan for their association to last.

Roxy was trying to put on a cheerful face as she and Jamie ate dinner alone at the huge dining table. Two other places had been set. One was for Hesper, who, Roxy had learned, lived in the caretaker's cottage on the property and often ate dinner with Tobias when her husband was away. The other was for Tobias. Both were locked in Tobias's study with orders that they were not to be disturbed.

Tobias had come out a while ago to inform her that Eric, Garth and Hagen had traced the man they were looking for to a local technical college. He'd told her not to worry and for her and Jamie to begin dinner without him and Hesper. He said Hesper was helping him trace the man's bank accounts. Roxy had offered to help in any way she could, but he'd told her they had the situation under control.

"Eric will catch the guy," Jamie said.

She knew from his tone that he was saying that as much to keep his own courage up as to try to make her feel better. The sound of footsteps caused her to look to the door to see Tobias and Hesper enter. Their expressions brought a rush of relief.

"No need for any further worry," Tobias announced cheerfully. "Eric and the two of you are both safe. Eric is no longer a threat to the man who ordered his death. Our villain has either perished in an accident or disappeared and will reemerge with a new face and a new identity. In case the latter is true, I shall be on the lookout for him. He shall be Dr. Moriarty to my Sherlock Holmes.''

''My vote is on you,'' Roxy said, noting the resolve in Tobias's eyes.

Tobias smiled broadly. ''I thank you for your faith in me.''

''When will Eric be back?'' Jamie asked.

''By morning,'' Tobias replied. ''I'm having Garth and Hagen remain in California to gather information, but since Eric is not yet officially a part of my organization, I've ordered him back.'' His gaze fell on Roxy. ''Besides, he has business here.''

Again the thought that Tobias had been merely humoring her until he could get Eric back occurred to her. And she wouldn't have blamed him if that was his ploy.

''Now eat up,'' Tobias ordered, pulling Hesper's chair out for her. ''Gretchen hates to see a good meal go to waste.''

With a forked bite midway to his mouth, Jamie paused. ''I guess that means we'll be going back to the farm as soon as Eric gets back.''

Roxy heard the edge of disappointment in his voice.

''Not immediately, I hope,'' Tobias replied. His gaze again turned on Roxy. ''Could I have a few minutes of your time following dinner?''

''Yes, of course,'' she replied, her appetite gone as she wondered if he was going to recommend a good psychiatrist.

Following the meal, Hesper challenged Jamie to a game on the computer. Roxy had the feeling this had been prearranged between Tobias and his grandniece. And because Hesper had not treated her any differently, she assumed the woman did not know the reason for the private interview.

As Hesper and Jamie left, Tobias rose and escorted Roxy into the sitting room. "Grace and Sam Carlson were killed in a car accident," he informed her when they were both seated. "They were survived by a daughter, Claire. She's six years old and in a hospital in Baltimore, Maryland. Following the accident, she was unconscious for several days. Now she's awake and on her way to a full recovery. There appears to be no immediate family to claim her. From what my investigator has been able to discover from neighbors, both parents were orphans. They met in the orphanage, fell in love and married. The social services people have been called in."

"She actually exists?" Roxy asked, finding this difficult to believe.

"Yes." Tobias's manner became fatherly. "And I think you should go see her. If you feel the same kind of attachment to her that you do to Jamie, I can arrange for you to adopt her."

The thought of having a reason to continue her liaison with Eric brought a surge of pleasure. In the next instant she scowled at herself. "I don't know if it would be fair to ask Eric to stick around for a second adoption."

"With the right connections, husbands are not always necessary," Tobias replied. "With or without him, I can arrange for you to have the child to raise."

"You would do that?"

"You have a lot of love to give, and the child needs that."

Roxy clasped her hands together in an effort to still their shaking. "To be honest, I'm a little scared. Actually, I'm a lot scared. It doesn't seem really possible that I could have a dream about a child I've never met."

"You heard Jamie crying out to you," Tobias reminded her.

Her chin tightened. "I have to see her."

Tobias smiled comfortingly. "I'll make the arrangements."

Chapter Eleven

Roxy woke as Eric entered the room. A joy spread through her, and a sense of wholeness as if her world was once again complete blanketed her. Her chin trembled. She didn't want to feel this bonded to him. It was only going to lead to hurt.

As he undressed in the dim predawn light, Eric breathed in the soft scent of shampoo and soap lingering in the air. He glanced to the bed to see Roxy's form beneath the covers. A crooked smile tilted one corner of his mouth. This sure beat coming back to an empty apartment. Abruptly the smile vanished. *Just don't get used to it!* his inner voice warned. Their paths were due to fork soon.

Roxy had intended to feign sleep, but when he joined her under the covers, she turned, yawned as if just then awaking and said, "I'm glad you're back safely."

"And I'm glad you and Jamie are safe." Her nearness had him already aroused. He kissed her shoulder and then her lips.

"You must be exhausted," she said, trying to show some restraint in preparation for their parting.

"I slept on the plane." He'd been nibbling her earlobe. Now he stopped. He wasn't certain if she was merely making conversation or if she was trying to politely tell him that she no longer wanted their intimacy to continue. It took all of his control, but he ordered himself to let her make the next move.

The heat of his body melted her desire to show resistance. Reasoning that she might as well enjoy his company while it lasted, she moved into his arms. "I'm glad to hear that."

Eric experienced a surge of male triumph. Hungry for the feel of her, he trailed his hands over her. When he came to the scarring, a protectiveness filled him. *She nearly got killed because of you,* he reminded himself curtly. The thought that the right thing for him to do would be to leave the bed now and make a clean break with her played through his mind. *One last time can't hurt,* he argued as she kissed his shoulder and ignited desire too strong to deny.

Roxy lay staring up at the ceiling. Outside the sun was fully up. Beside her, Eric was sleeping peacefully. Memories of their lovemaking returned, and the embers of passion that were always smoldering when he was present threatened to burst into flame.

No! she ordered her body. She needed to talk to him, to tell him about Claire Carlson. A nervousness swept through her. He was bound to think she was spooky and want to put as much distance between them as possible. But then, each of them going their own way had always been the plan.

Eric had woken quietly a couple of minutes earlier. Seeing the hard line of her jaw, he'd lain studying her covertly. He knew that look. She had something serious on her mind, something that was making her very uncomfortable. A part of him wanted to go back to sleep and put off the inevitable for a while longer. But he'd never been one to turn his back on the truth. "Looks like there's something we need to talk about," he said.

She jerked her gaze to him, to discover him studying her coolly. "It's a little difficult."

So the time for parting has come, he thought. He'd schooled himself to feel indifference. Instead, there was a sharp jab of pain. Ignoring it, he said dryly, "Let me save you the trouble. You and Jamie are going back to the farm today and you don't want any more trouble following you, so you'd prefer if I stayed behind." He shrugged as if this was of no consequence. "It's time I got back to work, anyway."

The ease with which he was accepting their parting stung. "Yes, that's it," she said stiffly, telling herself she should be relieved. Now there was no reason to tell him about Claire. Tobias had said he could arrange the adoption without Eric's help. Determined to end their relationship with dignity, she added, "I've enjoyed your company."

"I've enjoyed yours, too," he replied.

The urge to cry was strong and she realized she'd wanted him to beg her to stay. *This isn't the kind of life you want,* she chided herself. *You don't want a husband you have to worry about getting himself killed every time he goes off to work.* Angry with herself for letting emotions get involved, she slipped out of bed and headed into the bathroom.

Eric tried to go back to sleep, but he was too restless. He thought of her and Jamie alone on the farm. There were no neighbors in sight. They were easy prey for any nut who came along. "You're just looking for excuses to hang around in her life," he grumbled at himself. She'd done just fine on her own before he'd come along, he reminded himself curtly. Still, the worry persisted.

"When do you plan to leave?" he asked when she came out of the bathroom and began to dress.

"I'm not sure. Soon."

He'd expected her to say "On the next plane out." He studied her narrowly. She was being evasive. He'd let his emotions get involved and jumped to the conclusion that she'd wanted to talk about their parting. A bud of hope grew within him. Had he been wrong about her purpose? Maybe she wasn't so anxious to get rid of him as he'd thought. "There's something you're not telling me. You might as well spit it out. I'm a good detective. I'll find out sooner or later."

The set of his jaw told her that he was speaking the truth. *So what if he thinks you're weird?* she told herself. He was bowing out of her life forever, anyway. Finishing dressing, she turned to him, her shoulders stiff with dignity. "Do you remember my saying I heard a child sobbing down by the lake?"

The question surprised him. "Yes."

"Well, that night I dreamed about a sobbing child. A little girl. She was standing in front of two gravestones. I could read the names, Sam and Grace Carlson, and the dates of their births and deaths. I woke up and couldn't get the image out of my mind. I went downstairs. Tobias found me and I told him about the dream. He checked into the names and discovered that Mr. and Mrs. Carlson had recently been killed in an accident and their little girl was orphaned. So he's going to arrange for me to meet her." Her shoulders squared even more. "I know it sounds spooky, but that's the way it is."

For a long moment Eric was silent. He could see that she was scared. There had to be a reasonable explanation, he told himself. "Maybe you saw something about the accident on the news or read about it in the newspaper."

"Tobias suggested the same thing. But I'm pretty sure that's not the answer. The accident happened in Baltimore, Maryland. I wouldn't have seen any local news from there. Besides, a news report wouldn't have given their dates of birth."

Eric couldn't fault her logic, but that left one big question unanswered. "So how do you think you knew of this orphaned child?"

She drew a terse breath, then said levelly, "It's the same sixth sense that lets me read the Tarot cards and let me hear Jamie crying for me." An embarrassed flush built from her neck upward. "But don't worry. If Claire is the child I've been seeing and hearing, Tobias says he can arrange for me to adopt her without having to have a husband. Guess you'll be really relieved to see me getting out of your life now." Without waiting for a response, she left the room.

Eric lay back, his hands tucked under his head. So, not only did Roxy read Tarot cards but instead of the crying she heard before Jamie came into her life being a residual effect of the loss of her child, she believed she actually heard real children from hundreds of miles away.

"So everyone has their little eccentricities," he muttered, finding himself unwilling to label her as crazy. And he didn't like the idea of anyone else thinking that, either.

Leaving the bed, he got dressed and went in search of Tobias. He found him in his study. "I understand you've helped my wife locate a child."

"Yes." Tobias said nothing more. Instead, he watched Eric with an expectant expression and Eric knew he was waiting for him to reveal his feelings about the matter.

"I'm sure she heard about the child on a news broadcast or read about her in the paper and just forgot," Eric said.

"That is possible," Tobias conceded.

Eric breathed a sigh of relief. Tobias showed no indication he thought Roxy was one brick short of a full load. Clearly, he assumed she simply had an overactive imagination.

"On the other hand," Tobias said, "your wife could have amazingly strong maternal instincts and a very acutely developed sixth sense that some children can tap into."

Eric stared at him. The man was sincere. "You honestly believe that's possible?"

"I believe there are a great many things in this world that defy our usual understanding."

Eric had always held Tobias in the highest esteem. He didn't want to believe that the woman who'd grown to mean a great deal to him and the man he'd thought of as his mentor were both mentally unbalanced. "What you're suggesting is a little difficult to accept."

"Man is always seeking to unlock more of the mind. A great many people believe in ESP. Important universities fund studies in it. Countries—Russia, for example—have sought to develop it into a usable power. So much money. So much research. Surely there must be something to it," Tobias replied.

"I suppose you do have a point," Eric conceded.

"Think of it as a natural talent," Tobias suggested. "Some people are born with athletic ability, others with artistic skill, and still others with musical gifts. Who are we to put limits on what the mind can and can't do?''

The phone rang, interrupting their conversation. Hanging up a couple of minutes later, Tobias said, ''Claire Carlson is to be released from the hospital tomorrow. I'm going to arrange for Roxy to see her today. If the two hit it off, I'll arrange for the child to be released into Roxy's care. Would you like to accompany your wife, or do you find all of this too eerie to deal with?''

Eric had to admit to feeling unnerved by this situation. However, he needed to see for himself how Roxy and the child reacted to each other. ''I'll accompany her.''

A couple of hours later Roxy and Eric were on a plane bound for Baltimore. Jamie had remained behind in Tobias's care. When Roxy had told him that she might be bringing back a sister for him, Eric had noticed that the boy's response had been less than enthusiastic.

''I've heard sisters can be a real nuisance,'' Jamie had said.

Roxy had hugged him. ''I think she needs us.''

Jamie had looked resigned as he'd waved goodbye to them.

Sitting back in his seat, Eric studied Roxy covertly. The way she was chewing on her inner jaw told him that she was fighting a bout of nerves.

''I was surprised when I learned you were going to accompany me,'' she said, breaking the silence between them.

''I may be a skeptic, but you are my wife and, therefore, my responsibility,'' he replied, refusing to admit how much he wanted to be there with her.

Outwardly, she managed to show no emotion. Inwardly, a sharp jab of pain pierced her. She'd hoped he would say that he wanted to be there with her. In the next instant she was admonishing herself for this weakness. *Think separate lives!* she ordered herself. "I'm not your responsibility, nor have I ever been."

The thought that he would give his life for her flashed through his mind. "I feel like you are."

"Well, I'm not."

Still startled by how strongly he felt about protecting her, he said dryly, "We male chauvinist pigs have our own unique way of seeing the world. I can't change who or what I am."

She looked at the firm line of his jaw, and the thought that she liked him just the way he was played through her mind. *He doesn't want a family tying him down,* she reminded herself curtly and, allowing a silence to fall between them, turned her attention to the view beyond the window.

Eric wasn't certain what he expected to happen when he and Roxy entered Claire Carlson's room. On the way to the hospital Roxy had insisted on stopping at a toy store, where she'd purchased a stuffed turtle, a box of crayons and a coloring book.

Now as they entered the hospital, he sensed her increasing tension.

"My being here feels right," she said as they stood alone in the elevator. "But I have to admit I'm scared. The problem is I'm not certain what scares me most…that she will be the child I've been seeing or that she won't. If she isn't, then maybe I am nuts."

Again he experienced an overwhelming urge to protect her. Placing a comforting arm around her waist, he said firmly, "Everything's going to be all right."

His touch bolstered her courage. "I know you're not

any more certain of that than I am. But thanks for saying it."

"You see. We male chauvinist pigs are good for something," he quipped back.

She looked up at him, her gaze meeting his. "I do appreciate everything you've done for me."

The thought of her in his arms brought a huskiness to his voice. "I'm glad I could be of service."

Until now, she added silently as the elevator door opened on their floor and she saw his jaw tense as he looked down the hall.

The closer she came to the door of the room occupied by Claire Carlson, the stronger Roxy was drawn in its direction, until she felt almost as if there was a rope attached to her, dragging her there.

Eric saw the expression on her face intensifying and had the feeling that he'd been forgotten.

At the door of the room Roxy paused for a split second, took a deep breath, then entered. The child lying in the bed was the blond, blue-eyed girl from her dreams. "Hi," she said, smiling softly as she approached. "My name's Roxy."

Tears welled in the child's eyes. "Where have you been? I've been waiting for you. I was afraid you wouldn't come."

Roxy hid her shock behind a plastic smile. "You've been expecting me?"

"I dreamed about you." The tears in the six-year-old's eyes began to flow down her cheeks. "My mommy and daddy have gone to heaven and I've been so scared. They left me here all alone. I know they didn't want to. The doctor told me so. But they did."

"Sometimes people don't have a choice," Roxy soothed.

"I told the doctor I had to wait here until you came to take me home with you. He didn't believe me." A plea entered the teary blue eyes. "You have come to take me home with you, haven't you?"

Roxy wrapped her arms around the child. "Yes, I've come to take you home."

The child's sobbing increased with relief and Roxy held her more tightly. When Claire finally calmed and her crying subsided, Roxy released her and reached into the bag to pull out the stuffed turtle. "I brought you a few get-well gifts."

Claire's eyes rounded in surprise. "Raymond." Then she looked more closely and a frown spread over her face. "Not the real one. He hasn't been hugged enough and his tail is still new. The neighbor's dog chewed off my Raymond's tail and Mommy made him a new one." A fresh tear trickled down her cheek. "I guess the real Raymond has gone to heaven, too."

"You could think of this new turtle as Raymond's twin brother," Roxy suggested.

Claire looked hard at the green face. "Yes. He can be Ralph." The tears began to flow again as she hugged the turtle to her.

The woman and the child were not alike in appearance, Eric noted. Their facial features were different and Roxy's dark hair and eyes were in sharp contrast to the child's blond hair and blue eyes, yet for some reason he felt as if they belonged together. He'd remained at a distance from the bed and continued to remain there, uncertain of what he should do. Deciding that his role was to take care of business, he said, "I'll call Tobias and have him make the necessary arrangements."

As if just then realizing he was there, Claire abruptly ceased sobbing and looked past Roxy to him.

Eric had been scrutinized before, but never so openly or with such intensity. He smiled a crooked, encouraging smile.

"Is he coming with us?" Claire asked, not taking her eyes off him.

"Yes," Roxy replied, wondering how she would soothe the girl's fears if for some reason Eric's presence frightened her.

The child nodded her consent. "My mother always said it was nice to have a man around."

Feeling as if he'd just passed a very important test, Eric winked at her, then completed his exit. As he placed his call to Tobias, he wondered how many other children Roxy would be gathering to her nest. He pictured her surrounded by a dozen. Children, en masse, had always intimidated him. Only this time they didn't. This time he experienced what could only be described as a strong fatherly urge to care for them. "It would never work," he growled at himself. He shoved the images from his mind, and his expression hardened with purpose. The time had come for him and Roxy to part company.

Back in the hospital room, Claire frowned thoughtfully. "What's his name?"

"Eric," Roxy replied.

Claire looked at the ring on her finger. "Is he your husband?"

"For now."

Claire's frown turned to an expression of confusion.

"He has a very dangerous occupation. I want you to have a more stable environment."

Claire's frown returned. "I think he needs us."

Roxy hid her surprise. Jamie had said the same thing, and the cards had implied it. But she could not put the children at risk. "Eric Bishop is trained to look after himself," she said. Besides, he had Tobias to watch over him.

Claire didn't look convinced. Not wanting to continue this discussion, Roxy brought out the crayons and the coloring book.

Chapter Twelve

Roxy stood at the window of Tobias's study, looking out onto the back patio. She'd requested a meeting with him and was waiting for him to join her.

Yesterday she, Eric and Claire had arrived back at the estate. She knew Tobias was expecting them to remain for a while longer, but the time had come for her and the children to depart.

Ever since their return Eric had avoided her and the children. He'd tried to hide his evasion by claims of work that needed to be done. But she'd sensed his hesitancy to be with them and she knew Jamie had, as well. During dinner last night and again at breakfast this morning she'd seen the boy watching Eric with a puzzled expression on his face.

And if she needed further proof, there was last night. Eric hadn't slept in their bed. He'd told her he would be working late. This morning he'd come in while she was dressing and said he'd fallen asleep on the couch in the computer room, but she hadn't been fooled. She'd known he'd planned it that way. The memory of her realization that he no longer wanted to share her bed caused a pain so intense it brought a threatened flood of tears to her eyes. *You knew this day would come,* she admonished herself curtly.

Determinedly pushing him from her mind, she focused her attention on her two children. They were seated at the table on the patio. Knowing how cautious Jamie was to make friends with other children, she'd expected his acceptance of Claire to take some time. But almost immediately upon their return, Jamie had assumed the role of big brother. "She needs us," he'd said simply, and that had been their entire discussion about Claire joining their family.

A soft smile of motherly love spread over her face. Jamie was showing Claire how to use the laptop computer Tobias had purchased for him. Suddenly the young girl sat back in her chair and stared off into the distance. Roxy's smile vanished. She knew what had happened. It had happened several times before. The grief Claire was working her way through had again become overwhelming, claiming her mind and her emotions.

Forgetting that she was waiting for Tobias, Roxy started to exit through the French doors when she saw Jamie stop playing on the computer and take the girl's hand in his. Claire looked up at him and he gave her an encouraging smile. Although she didn't smile back, she did continue to hold on to his hand while using her free hand to wipe away the tears streaming down her cheeks. Her gaze again turned to the tree line in the distance, but the flow of tears had become a trickle.

That Jamie seemed to know instinctively how to comfort his newfound sister amazed Roxy. That Claire accepted his comfort pleased her.

"You asked to see me?" Tobias's voice broke into her thoughts.

"Yes." She turned to face him. "I appreciate your hospitality, but it's time for Claire, Jamie and me to be going home."

"I was hoping you would remain longer," he coaxed.

"You're very kind, but Claire needs to be settled into a steady environment as soon as possible."

"In that case, I have a proposal for you." Picking up the phone, Tobias punched one of the in-house extension numbers. "However, I feel it would be only fair for Eric to be present when I present it."

Roxy wanted to refuse. Eric Bishop no longer wanted to be a part of her life and she had no desire for him to be involved in any decisions she made. But before she could protest, Tobias was giving orders to send Eric to his study.

The sudden worry that Tobias might be considering playing matchmaker caused a rush of panic. That would only lead to embarrassment. She had to nip that notion in the bud. "Eric didn't enter this marriage with any long-term plans," she said when Tobias hung up. "If he's involved in any proposal you're considering, I'm sure he'll have no interest in it. And it wouldn't be fair to even ask him to participate."

"I'm not intending to propose that the two of you remain married," he assured her.

"Then I don't understand why he has to be here." Until this moment she hadn't realized how hurt she was that Eric hadn't learned to care for her. Silently, she mocked herself. Why should he have? She'd chosen to maintain an emotional barrier between them, never giving any indication that she wanted anything other than a short-term arrangement with him. She had, in fact, made it very clear he was not what she considered either suitable husband material for her nor father material for her children.

Of course, he hadn't made any attempt to break down that barrier, either, she mused coldly. *It's unfair, even irrational, for you to have expected him to,* her reasonable side rebutted. She'd been the one to propose to him. He hadn't come looking for a wife and instant family. Still, unwanted and unwarranted anger toward him built within her. The fear of losing control spread through her. She didn't want him there while Tobias made his proposal. When Eric had returned to their bedroom this morning looking like a rumpled blanket, she'd had to fight hard not to make some dry remark about him not coming to their bed during the night. If he made any comment about her future, she wasn't certain if she could keep herself from taking a sharp jab at him that might expose the pain she was feeling.

"I would not feel right speaking to you about your future without Eric present. Currently he is your husband," Tobias insisted.

"Our marriage isn't—" Her protest was cut short by a knock on the door, followed by Eric's entrance.

Eric looked from Roxy to Tobias, his expression polite, betraying no emotion. "Can I assume you and Roxy have been talking about her travel plans?" He expected to feel relieved that she would be going. Instead, this thought made him uneasy.

Just stay cool! she ordered herself. "Tobias insisted you be here," she said, letting him know that she had not sought his presence. "I told him that what the children and I did was no longer your concern."

Eric could almost feel the carving knife slicing through him as she cut him out of her life. *This is what you wanted,* he reminded himself. *Well, maybe not entirely anymore,* he amended. "I don't intend to interfere in yours or the children's lives, but I do intend to check on you and them periodically. I want to know that all of you are safe, and I will aid you financially." These thoughts had been tormenting him all day. He'd argued that she would fight him and, for the sake of peace, he should make a clean break. But now that he'd spoken them aloud, he knew they were a pledge he would live up to no matter how much she protested.

She was going to tell him that she required nothing from him when Tobias interrupted. "The two of you can work out whatever details you want later. For the moment, I want the floor." He motioned toward the two chairs facing his desk. As they sat down, he rounded the desk.

Seating himself, he regarded Roxy in a businesslike manner. "The farmhouse requires a great deal more work than a mere dressing up. However, if you insist on returning there, I'll pay for new wiring, new plumbing and whatever else is required."

Her back stiffened with pride. She didn't like being an object of charity. "I appreciate your offer, but I'm sure we'll be just fine."

Ignoring her protest, Tobias continued. "Also, if you return to the farm, you'll have to go back to work, and that will require finding someone to look after the children. That disturbs me. You are the one best qualified to care for them."

"I don't like it, either, but life isn't perfect," she returned, preparing to refuse his offer of further charity.

"And who knows what fate has in store? There could be more children who cry out to you."

This possibility had occurred to Roxy, but she'd decided that worrying about it would do no good. "If that happens, I'll deal with it."

Tobias's expression became stern. "On this point I will not take no for an answer. You'll notify me and I'll help you find the child and bring him or her into your family."

Knowing she didn't have the resources to fight the legal system, she nodded her consent. "I would appreciate your help in that instance."

So Tobias also thought there might be more children. Mentally, Eric patted himself on the back. His image of Roxy surrounded by a bevy of children could easily be right on the mark. And he didn't belong in that kind of group picture. But even as he told himself that, he couldn't erase the puzzlement and the pain of rejection he'd seen in Jamie's eyes this morning, nor the hollow feeling that had been haunting him all day. He was doing what both he and Roxy knew was the right thing, he told himself sternly.

"And now to my proposal." Tobias's gaze narrowed on Roxy with purpose. "Hesper and Garth are talking of having a family. And I have other employees who would benefit from a day-care facility housed here on the estate. If you would consider running it for me, I'll build you a house on the grounds so that you may have a private residence for yourself and your children. This will allow you to earn a living and be with your children, as well. The day-care facility will be built onto the house so that the parents can visit with their children during the day and assure themselves that their offspring are happy and well cared for. There might also be times when you would be required to keep the children overnight or for a couple of days. You will, of course, be well compensated for your work."

Roxy had to admit the offer appealed to her. There was just one catch. Eric. Their marriage was over. She'd accepted that. But it wasn't easy to think of being alone once again. And no matter how often she told herself that he led too dangerous a life, she wasn't certain she could make herself stop wishing she was still sharing it.

Tobias rose. "I'll leave the two of you to discuss my offer."

Roxy waited until the door was closed, then said, "Tobias's offer is generous. However, I think it would be best if the children and I went back to the farm."

Eric frowned. In his mind's eye he again pictured the farm...isolated, several miles out of town away from help. "I think you should stay here. The estate is secure, safe. The children would be under Tobias's protection." He'd risen and moved to the window. From there he could see Jamie and Claire. The shadow of pain that always seemed to be in the little girl's eyes tore at him. "And he's right. Claire, especially, needs you full-time right now."

Roxy studied his ramrod-straight back. "I wouldn't want you to feel that I was impinging on your life. That wasn't our agreement."

Eric's frown darkened. She was willing to refuse Tobias's generous offer just to put distance between him and her. Schooling the frown from his face, he turned to her, his expression politely friendly. "I'll sleep better at night knowing you and the children are safe. As for our paths continually crossing, you don't have to worry about that. I won't be here. Tobias has recently received a request from a very wealthy businessman in Zurich, Switzerland, to provide security for himself and his family. It will mean living in his home and traveling with him. I'm going to volunteer to take that assignment."

Roxy scowled. "There is no reason for you to travel halfway around the world just to get away from me."

He smiled dryly. "You've got that a little backward, don't you? It's you who wants to get away from me."

His jaw tensed. That had sounded as if he wanted to stay with her. His shoulders squared with pride. He'd learned early in life never to ask to remain where he wasn't wanted. Besides, hadn't he already determined that being a father to a bevy of children wasn't for him? Erasing the emotion from his face, he added with indifference, "Either way, it doesn't matter. The truth is, I like Europe, and seeing it from the socially elite's point of view will be fun." Putting an end to the discussion, he left.

"I'm sure it will," she replied to his departing back, picturing him looking handsome and in command as he stood guard. She guessed he would not be lonely on those cold alpine nights, either. Again a sharp jab of pain pierced her. Resolve etched itself into her face. For the umpteenth time she told herself that her children did not need for a father figure, a man who led the kind of life Eric Bishop led...never knowing how long he would be gone each time he left the house or if he would be returning alive.

Restless, she rose and went out onto the patio. "Tobias has offered me a job," she informed Jamie and Claire. "How would you feel about remaining here permanently?"

Jamie smiled and nodded. "I like it here."

Claire simply nodded.

Relief spread across Jamie's features. "I know Eric is going to start working for Tobias, too. Was he afraid we wouldn't want to stay? Is that why he's been staying away from me and Claire? Are we all going to be a real family now?"

"You, Claire and I are a real family," Roxy replied, taking a hand of each child in one of hers. "Eric won't be staying here."

Claire had been looking past her, toward the house. "He'll be lonely without us," she said.

Roxy looked in the direction the child had been looking and saw Eric watching them, a cold, distant expression on his face. "I doubt that very much."

"He will," Claire declared.

"I thought we were a team," Jamie insisted, disappointment strong in his voice.

"I'm trying to do what is best for all of us," Roxy replied.

They didn't look convinced, but both nodded their acceptance.

Roxy stood in her shower, the water cascading over her. She'd kept busy with the children all day. In the afternoon they'd taken a long walk around the grounds. Tobias had joined them and showed them where he would build the house for them if they agreed to stay. Roxy had told him that they would. Now it was late, the children were asleep and she was left with her thoughts.

Her gaze went to her scarring. Truths she'd been avoiding flooded in on her. Wanting Eric Bishop out of her life because he might bring danger to her and the children was no longer a real fear. She knew they were safe now and that Tobias and Eric would always see that they remained that way. As for Eric continually putting his life in jeopardy, a lot of men did that—policemen, firemen. Life was never guaranteed, no matter what a person did. An accountant could die in a car crash on his way to the office. Breathing a tired sigh, she admitted that she continued to refuse to consider a life with him because of other fears she hadn't wanted to face.

Turning off the water, she toweled dry and pulled on a

nightgown. She knew what she wanted to do, but she lacked the courage.

Her gaze went to the box holding her Tarot cards. Retrieving the deck, she sat on the bed. She read them first for Eric and then for herself. The readings only made her more nervous. "Maybe I'm interpreting the cards the way I want to interpret them and not the way they're meant to be interpreted," she muttered.

It wouldn't be the first time she'd done that. The image of her ex-husband came into her mind and a bitter taste filled her mouth. In that instance, her reading hadn't really been a misinterpretation, she reminded herself. The cards had warned her that he had his faults. But she'd loved him and had been willing to overlook them.

What she needed, she told herself, was a good night's sleep. Tomorrow she'd read the cards again, then decide what to do. Putting the deck away, she climbed into bed. But sleep wouldn't come. Giving in to her restlessness, she rose and, leaving the room dark, went to the window. Below, leaning against the trunk of an ancient oak, was a man. He was in the shadows, but she knew it was Eric.

She hadn't seen him since their meeting in Tobias's study. He hadn't eaten lunch or dinner with her and the children. Tobias had explained that Eric was in the briefing room helping sort out the clues on a puzzling case, but they all knew that was only an excuse. He was cutting the bond with them, fully and completely.

She told herself to go back to bed. Instead she remained, hungry for the sight of him as if it gave her life.

Below, Eric saw the slender form half-hidden by the curtain. He'd been standing there staring up at Roxy's window ever since she'd gone to her room. Last night had been difficult. Today had been hell. He was doing what he knew she wanted and what he told himself he wanted, as well. So why did he feel so ripped apart inside?

He saw a flutter and knew she'd left the window. He shifted his gaze to the night sky. A wry smile tilted the corners of his mouth. So maybe he didn't like being the lone wolf any longer. Maybe it was time he looked for a wife, one who could live with his life-style. Roxy's image filled his mind. A scowl of frustration spread over his face. *Forget her!* he ordered himself.

"I thought it was you out here." Roxy's voice broke into his thoughts.

He blinked, for a moment wondering if he'd been thinking about her so hard he'd conjured up a visual image of her. Shaking off this ridiculous notion, he let his gaze travel over her. Even in her old robe and scruffy slippers she looked sexier than any woman he'd ever known. "Just thought I'd get a breath of fresh air before turning in."

Suddenly realizing she needed a reason for being there, she said, "I wasn't certain we would get a chance to be alone before you left, so I thought I'd take this opportunity to thank you for all you've done."

"You're welcome." So this was how it was to end...a quiet thank-you and goodbye. Wanting to assure her that he understood completely, he said, "Mrs. Gibbons fixed me up a room in the east wing."

The urge to reach out and touch him was close to overwhelming. Until this moment she had not admitted how much even the slightest physical contact seemed to fill her with joy. But the protective shield she'd built around herself was not yet ready to crumble. "Jamie missed you today." Recalling the way Claire had seemed to always notice Eric when he was anywhere in sight, she added, "And Claire as well, I believe."

It irked him that she hadn't included herself. *She's just*

made it clear she's glad to be saying goodbye, he chided himself. "I missed them." His jaw hardened. "I know you want the break to be complete, but before I leave I intend to tell them that if they ever need me, all they have to do is tell Tobias and I'll show up." He'd meant to stop there, but couldn't. In stiff tones, he added, "The same goes for you. I know we're not family nor will we ever be, but you and the children are the closest I've ever come to that so far."

Roxy chewed nervously on her inner cheek. In spite of the apparent ease with which he'd distanced himself from her and the children, he wasn't ready to write them or her off entirely. She could take that as an encouraging sign. *Trust your instincts! Take a chance!* her inner voice commanded. She'd done that once before, she rebutted. *Okay, so approach it slowly. Don't just give up and turn tail and run,* it returned. She drew a shaky breath. She could do that. "I read your cards tonight and then I read mine."

Surprised by this change of direction in their conversation, Eric studied her narrowly. "And what did they say?"

Mentally she congratulated herself. This was a good ploy...a safe one. She would let the cards speak and see what his reaction was. "They said that you and I and the children belong together." She'd meant to say this casually. Instead her nervousness caused it to come out curtly.

Obviously she hadn't been pleased with the reading, Eric mused acidly. "You make that sound like a fate worse than death." She was making their break a great deal easier, but he'd had enough of this conversation. He straightened away from the tree. "On that note, I think I'll say good-night."

"Wait, please," she blurted, furious with herself. "I didn't mean it that way."

He frowned impatiently. "How did you mean it?" Immediately he wished he'd just kept going. She was probably going to say something about friendship and he was in no mood for that. Grudgingly he confessed that he'd let his emotions get involved...too involved.

"Sometimes the cards tell people what they don't want to hear. I wasn't so sure you'd want to know what they said."

"Are we talking about me or are we talking about you?" he asked coldly.

"Maybe both." He hadn't given her any sign that he cared. *I'm setting myself up to be humiliated,* she thought frantically. She couldn't face that again. "My coming out here wasn't such a good idea." She turned to leave.

Eric saw her chin tremble and read the fear in her eyes. Had he misinterpreted her motives? He caught her arm, forcing her to remain. "I'm not opposed to the idea of having a family," he confessed gruffly.

She fought back a fresh rush of panic. It was time to ask the big question. "Your own biological offspring or a wayward band of collected children who have no place else to go?"

He remembered her history and knew the pain this question was causing her. "There are enough children in this world who need parents without my adding to the number."

She heard the honesty in his voice, but still she was afraid to believe him. "Are you sure about that?"

"Yes." Was this the real reason she'd been so determined to keep a distance between them? he wondered.

"You might change your mind."

The urge to take her in his arms and assure her that she didn't have to fear that came close to overpowering him. In that instant he knew he loved her. But she hadn't mentioned love to him. He would jump to no conclusions. "That would depend on what was being offered. Or if we're even talking about an offer."

She had guarded her heart too long. Even now she couldn't make herself completely bare her soul. "The children are very attached to you and you seem to have good natural fathering instincts. We could try to stay a family."

"For their sake only?" Her refusal to include herself as a reason for his remaining cut deep. Realizing he was still holding on to her arm, he released her. "I don't think so."

She felt suddenly more alone than she'd ever felt in her life. "For my sake, as well," she confessed, her voice barely above a whisper. "I feel incomplete without you."

Her words were like music to his ears, but the difficulty she'd had in saying them dampened his pleasure. Then a thought he didn't like at all occurred to him. "Are you sure you're not being unduly influenced by your cards?"

Roxy shook her head. "No. I knew before I read them how I felt. The truth is I was hoping they would say something different, something that would free me."

His impatience again surfaced. "Is it so bad to want to be with me?"

Tears welled in her eyes. "I don't want to suffer the kind of rejection I suffered before. I know nothing in this world is guaranteed, especially where the heart is concerned. I'm afraid of taking a chance."

"If I told you that I'd been standing down here staring up at your window, hating the thought of never seeing you again, would that ease your mind?"

Hope mingled with joy. "You have?"

Caressingly, he traced the line of her jaw with the tips of his fingers. "Life feels hollow without you and the children." His voice hardened. "But I can't change who I am or what I do."

She saw the plea for understanding in his eyes, and what was left of her resistance vanished. "I know. I also know that the children and I will be safe here. As for you and me and them, together we have more strength than each of us apart. I can't be certain that will keep you from harm, but I'm willing to take the chance and be grateful for any time we have together."

"I love you, Roxy," he said, crushing her to him.

"I love you, too," she replied, her lips finding his.

*   *   *   *   *

Take 4 bestselling love stories FREE

Plus get a FREE surprise gift!

As seen on TV!
Free Gift Offer

With a Free Gift proof-of-purchase from any Silhouette® book,
you can receive a beautiful cubic zirconia pendant.

This gorgeous marquise-shaped stone is a genuine cubic
zirconia—accented by an 18" gold tone necklace.

(Approximate retail value $19.95)

Send for yours today...
compliments of ▼ *Silhouette*®
TM

To receive your free gift, a cubic zirconia pendant, send us one original proof-of-
purchase, photocopies not accepted, from the back of any Silhouette Romance™,
Silhouette Desire®, Silhouette Special Edition®, Silhouette Intimate Moments®
or Silhouette Yours Truly™ title available at your favorite retail outlet, together with
the Free Gift Certificate, plus a check or money order for $1.65 U.S./$2.15 CAN. (do
not send cash) to cover postage and handling, payable to Silhouette Free Gift Offer.
We will send you the specified gift. Allow 6 to 8 weeks for delivery. Offer good until
December 31, 1997, or while quantities last. Offer valid in the U.S. and Canada only.

Free Gift Certificate

Name: _____

Address: _____

City: _____ State/Province: _____ Zip/Postal Code: _____

Mail this certificate, one proof-of-purchase and a check or money order for postage
and handling to: SILHOUETTE FREE GIFT OFFER 1997. In the U.S.: 3010 Walden
Avenue, P.O. Box 9077, Buffalo NY 14269-9077. In Canada: P.O. Box 613, Fort Erie,
Ontario L2Z 5X3.

FREE GIFT OFFER   084-KFD
ONE PROOF-OF-PURCHASE
To collect your fabulous FREE GIFT, a cubic zirconia pendant, you must include this
original proof-of-purchase for each gift with the properly completed Free Gift Certificate.

084-KFDR

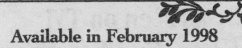
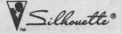